Thomas Vernon, Sidney Smith Rider

The Diary of Thomas Vernon

A Loyalist, Banished from Newport by the Rhode Island General Assembly in 1776

Thomas Vernon, Sidney Smith Rider

The Diary of Thomas Vernon
A Loyalist, Banished from Newport by the Rhode Island General Assembly in 1776

ISBN/EAN: 9783744728690

Printed in Europe, USA, Canada, Australia, Japan

Cover: Foto ©Raphael Reischuk / pixelio.de

More available books at **www.hansebooks.com**

RHODE ISLAND

HISTORICAL TRACTS.

NO. 13.

PROVIDENCE
SIDNEY S. RIDER.
1881.

PROVIDENCE PRESS COMPANY, PRINTERS

THE DIARY

OF

THOMAS VERNON

A LOYALIST

BANISHED FROM NEWPORT BY THE RHODE ISLAND
GENERAL ASSEMBLY IN 1776.

WITH NOTES BY SIDNEY S. RIDER.

TO WHICH IS ADDED

THE VERNON FAMILY AND ARMS,

AND THE

GENEALOGY OF RICHARD GREENE,

OF POTOWOMUT.

PROVIDENCE, R. I.
SIDNEY S. RIDER.
1881.

HISTORICAL INTRODUCTION.

———◆———

At the breaking out of the war of the Revolution, the Colony of Rhode Island found many of its inhabitants loyal to the Crown of Great Britain. This was particularly the case with the inhabitants of Newport. In that town resided many of those persons holding office under the Crown. A great majority of these persons remained loyal to the Crown, and thereby became obnoxious to the friends of the Colonies. Among those specially obnoxious, were the officers of the Vice Admiralty Court, and the Customs' officers. These antipathies broke out into absolute riot in 1765 at Newport, and in 1772, resulted in the destruction of the Gaspee, and the shooting of Lieut. Dudingston, her commander.

For the purpose of finding out who were her friends, and who her enemies, the Assembly passed an act at its June session, 1776, which became known as the Test Act. This extraordinary piece of legislation empowered any member of the Assembly who suspected his neighbor of being unfriendly to the cause of the United American Colonies, to summon such neighbor before him, and demand that he should subscribe to the Declaration, or Test. This Declaration, or Test, is in the following words:

"I, the subscriber, do solen..ly and sincerely declare, that I believe the War, Resistance, and Opposition, in which the United American Colonies are now engaged against the Fleets and Armies of Great Britain, is on the part of said Colonies just and necessary; and that I will not directly, nor indirectly, afford assistance of any sort or kind whatever to the said Fleets and Armies during the continuance of the present war; but I will heartily assist in the defence of the United Colonies."* There were eighty-two members of the Assembly, and as every one of these members could order his neighbors before him, there was thus erected in the State eighty-two petty courts of inquiry capable of becoming a source of the greatest annoyance to many people.

Upon the refusal of the suspected persons, so summoned to appear, and subscribe to the Test, the member of the Assembly was authorized to enquire into his reasons for not subscribing. If these reasons were unsatisfactory to the member, he was authorized and directed to issue a warrant directing the sheriff, or his deputy, to institute a search of the dwelling of the suspected persons, for arms or munitions of war. Thereupon the member was to make return of his proceedings to the next Assembly. Among the first persons arrested under this act were the five gentlemen whose story is told in the following Diary: Messrs. Thomas Vernon, Richard Beale, John Nicoll, Nicholas Lechmere, and Walter Chaloner. These five men are the only ones mentioned by Arnold in his History of Rhode Island, as having been arrested and exiled; but in truth there were many more. In July, eleven were exiled, besides whom there were

* Acts and Resolves, R. I. General Assembly, June, 1776, p. 100.

four Scotch officers, whose names are lost, and doubtless many others.

Notwithstanding there is nothing contained in the act prescribing banishment, or punishment of any kind, yet these men were immediately banished from Newport. The proceedings were summary. The Assembly met on the 10th of June. The act probably passed about the 15th, and on the 20th, four of the men were taken by the sheriff from Newport. The Test is on the 109th page of the Schedule, the banishment is on the 112th page of the same Schedule. It will thus be seen that the sentence was almost simultaneous with the passage of the Test. A more arbitrary proceeding it would be difficult to conceive. It was entirely without the sanction of law, the law being, as before stated, without penalty. Several weeks after these proceedings, these men having in the meantime been confined, the Assembly passed another act whereby certain pecuniary burdens were imposed. This law was clearly retro-active in its operation, and ought to have been of no effect. Among the first acts of the first Assembly in 1647, was one declaring that no citizen should be punished, " except by some known law." Nevertheless, these men were so punished. In October following, the Assembly passed an act giving permission to all banished persons to return to their homes, upon the payment by them of such expenses as the State had incurred. Thus for four months these unhappy men were kept wandering about the northerly towns of the State to the great discomfort of themselves, and of everybody with whom they came in contact.

The Diary of Mr. Vernon was recently privately printed, fifty copies only, by Thomas Vernon, Esq., of New York city; and it

is by his permission that it here again appears. The former
edition was entirely without notes, and many passages were
omitted. Many of these passages were trivial repetitions, notwithstanding which they have all been restored, for they at least
show the method and care of the Diarist. In the present edition
such laws as were connected with the events have been inserted
in their proper places, and such illustrative notes as were
required have been added. Extended biographical notices of
Henry Ward, Secretary, Gov. Jabez Bowen, Gov. William West,
and others, have been introduced. These notices contain mate-
rials not heretofore gathered in their proper connections.
Advantage has been taken of a reference to the Trial of the
Pirates, to introduce an account of that transaction, because
heretofore every account which has been given, from Arnold
back, has incorrectly stated the number of pirates hanged.
There were twenty-eight, instead of twenty-six, as is usually
stated.

The Diary gives us a picture of life in one of the inland towns
of the State during the Revolutionary period; the families, the
men, and the opinions are more or less referred to, and thus a
unique, curious, and hitherto unwritten chapter of Rhode Island
history is presented.

Following the Diary has been reprinted from the New England
Historical and Genealogical Register for July, 1879, a communi-
cation on the Vernon Family and Arms, by Harrison Ellery, of
Boston, with additions and corrections by Thomas Vernon, of
New York city. Taking advantage of a note concerning Richard
Greene, of Potowomut, the editor has introduced the Genealogy
of that family, for which he is indebted to Gen. George Sears
Greene, of Coweset.

THE DIARY.

———◆———

Thursday, June 20, 1776.   Pursuant to the order
of the General Assembly,[1] at four o'clock p. m., John

1. WHEREAS, Messieurs Richard Beale, John Nicoll, Nicholas Lechmere,
Thomas Vernon and Walter Chaloner having been examined before this
Assembly, and refused to subscribe the Test (see introduction) ordered by this
Assembly to be tendered to suspected persons; and it appearing that while
they continue in the principles by them avowed before this Assembly, they are
justly to be deemed unfriendly to the United Colonies; it is therefore

VOTED AND RESOLVED, That the Sheriff of the County of Newport forthwith remove the said Richard Beale, John Nicoll, Nicholas Lechmere and
Thomas Vernon to the town of Glocester in this Colony, where they shall be
permitted to go at large within the limits of the town, they giving their parole
of honor to continue there until further orders from this Assembly. That if
either of them shall forfeit his parole, he shall, upon being apprehended, be
committed to Gaol and kept closely confined until further orders from this
Assembly;—and that in case either of them shall refuse to give his parole
as aforesaid, he shall be confined to such House in the said town of Glocester as
the said Sheriff shall think fit, with liberty of the farm whereon the House
stands; and

WHEREAS, The said Sheriff hath in his hands several Executions against
the said Walter Chaloner, which are soon returnable, and upon which he is
now in the custody of the said Sheriff; it is therefore further

VOTED AND RESOLVED, That as soon as the said Walter Chaloner shall be

Nicoll,[1] Nicholas Lechmere,[2] Richard Beale,[3] and Thomas Vernon[4] were escorted by the Sheriff of the

discharged from the said Executions the said Sheriff immediately remove him to the said town of Glocester, in manner as the said Richard Beale and others are ordered to be removed, and under the like conditions and restrictions. (Acts and Resolves, R. I. Gen. Assem., June, 1776, p. 112.)

Mr. Chaloner never joined the party.

1. John Nicoll was Comptroller of Customs at Newport, under the Crown, from (at least) 1761 to 1775. At the time of the Stamp Act Riot in August, 1765, he, together with two other Customs officers, fled the town and took refuge on board the Cygnet man-of-war, then lying in the Harbor. From this ship they addressed Governor Ward a letter demanding protection. The Governor at once assured them of protection, and they returned to their duties. On the 16th September, 1776, Mr. Vernon parted company with Mr. Nicoll, leaving him confined in the Jail at Providence. This is the last we learn of him.

2. Nicholas Lechmere was technically known as Searcher, in the Customs at Newport; he was on board the Cygnet with Mr. Nicoll, as mentioned in the preceding note. There appear to have been several brothers by this name living in Newport, all of whom became more or less involved in the troubles of the times. In 1780 Mr. Lechmere removed to Bristol, England.

3. Richard Beale had long been a resident of Newport, having been admitted a freeman in 1757. He was a brother-in-law of Mr. Vernon, having married Miss Mary Brown, daughter of John Brown, Esq., of Newport.

4. Mr. Thomas Vernon, the author of the following Diary, was the son of Samuel Vernon, Esq., of Newport. He was born May 31, 1718, married September 9, 1741, to Jane, daughter of John Brown, a merchant of Newport. She died April 28, 1765. Mr. Vernon next married, May 20, 1766, Mrs Mary Mears. She died August, 1787. Mr. Vernon was postmaster of Newport under the British Government from 1745 to 1775. He was register of the Court of Admiralty for twenty years; was secretary of the Redwood Library eighteen years, and was senior warden of Trinity Church; he died in Newport May 1, 1784.

County of Newport[1] and his deputy, to the wharf of
Colonel Wanton, at the Point, where we embarked
on board of one William Greene's boat for the town
of East Greenwich, about twenty miles distant,
where we arrived about seven o'clock the same
evening, and were conducted to the house of one
Mr. Arnold, where we continued in custody of the
said Sheriff that night.

Friday, June 21, 1776. We arose early in the
morning in order to attend the Sheriff's further orders. We soon found that he met with much diffi-
culty in providing horses, etc. However, about ten
o'clock A. M., was brought to the door an old, crazy
chaise with a very bad horse, and two led horses
quite as indifferent. Mr. Beale was placed in the
chaise, and Mr. Nicoll and Mr. Lechmere on horseback. [In this way] we proceeded on our journey
with the Sheriff and his deputy. The weather being
very sultry, we made no stop until we arrived at
Brown's Furnace,[2] about twelve or fourteen miles

1. Jabez Champlin was Sheriff of Newport County.

2. There was at this time, and for several years previously there had been
mined, at a locality subsequently and to this day, known as the Ore Bed in
Cranston, a considerable quantity of iron ore. Another mine was on the north

distant, where got some refreshment. The people
of the house treated us with civility. We tarried
here about one hour. After shifting our horses we
proceeded on our journey through a very rocky
country and were much fatigued. We arrived at
the town of Glocester[1] about eleven o'clock at night
and lodged at the house of one Mr. Willmut (Wilmarth[2]), a publick inn.

bank of the Pawtuxet river. It had been discovered in the spring of 1765. A
company was formed comprised of Stephen and Rufus Hopkins, Jabez Bourn,
and Nicholas, Joseph, John and Moses Brown, for the purpose of operating
the mine. They wished to maintain a permanent dam without providing (as
by law they were required to do) a fish way. They petitioned the Assembly (a
similar petition by James Greene and others on the south bank of the Pawtuxet had been granted in 1741) and obtained permission. This petition
represents that the petitioners had, at vast expense, purchased a bank of ore,
erected a large furnace, purchased great tracts of woodland, laid out roads,
and been at great expense in various ways for the purpose of carrying on the
business of smelting the ore and making it into pigs. So many of the Browns
being interested in the enterprise, that it was doubtless known as Brown's
Furnace. It was subsequently the Hope Furnace.

1. The town of Glocester as originally laid out was twelve miles square.
It extended from the seven mile line on the east to the Connecticut line on the
west. It was the most northerly town in the State. It was taken from Providence in 1730-1. At the period of Mr. Vernon's banishment it was the third
town in the State, in point of population, ranking next Providence. In 1806
the town was divided in the centre by a line running east and west, making
two towns. The northerly one was called Burrillville and the southerly one
retaining the name of Glocester.

2. Stephen Wilmarth here referred to was the son of Captain Timothy

Saturday, June 22, 1776. We tarried at this house all day, and were much pleased with the conversation of the landlord. He appears to be a very sensible, intelligent man and very moderate in his sentiments, which afforded us much pleasure. He has sustained many public offices in this town, and we are told to satisfaction. We tarried at this house until about six o'clock in the evening, when the Sheriff and his deputy conducted us to the house of one Mr. Stephen Keetch[1] (Keach), about two miles distant, where we are detained till further orders, having refused to give our Parole to the Sheriff for liberty of ye town. The man of the

Wilmarth, a prominent tavern keeper (in these days tavern keepers were very important men) on the highway from Providence to Hartford, about six miles from the former town. Stephen married Nancy, daughter of James Aldrich, Esq.

1. Stephen Keach was a respectable farmer, living on a farm a little south of the center of the town of Glocester as it was then laid out. Mr. Keach's farm comprised about five hundred acres of land. The family consisted of seven persons—Mr. and Mrs. Keach, three sons, Stephen (the eldest), Christopher and Jeremiah, and two daughters, Freelove and Patty. There was a third daughter, probably older, and married; she is mentioned in the Diary under the date of July 21, and in other places as their daughter Winsor. Besides these people the family comprised two hired men, Christopher and Nicholas, and a hired boy, Joseph. The distances given to various points in the Diary, are to the Chepachet river two miles, to Chestnut Hill meeting-house nine miles, to Providence twelve miles.

house and his family received us kindly. They appear to be very plain, quiet, inoffensive people, and willing to oblige us. We supped on bread and milk, and retired to bed after nine. The lodging is as good as this country affords.

Sunday, June 23, 1776. Arose about five o'clock. The breakfast prepared being coffee. But I chose some whey. Afterwards walked out about two miles to view the river or stream where is a saw mill. The farm contains about five hundred acres of land, four-fifths of which appears to be uncultivated. One of our company having a few limes, we made a drink of punch. Our dinner prepared was salt pork and dried beans and corn. We diverted ourselves in reading and chatting until evening. Drank some milk and retired to bed about nine o'clock.

Monday, June 24, 1776. I arose about five o'clock, and the company about six o'clock. Amused ourselves in chatting till breakfast, which was coffee, but I chose milk. Mr. Nicoll, one of our company, prepared a small piece of ground and sowed some lettuce, spinnach, and other seeds. The land I find is

much parched for want of rain. Our dinner, salt
pork and a small piece of salt beef, with dried beans
and corn boiled, but one of our company picked
some wild herbs which, when boiled, made the salt
meat relish much better. We do not find any vege-
tables in the country of any kind, neither do we
apprehend we shall meet with any, which is a circumstance very disagreeable to us. However, the
civility of the family makes ample amends for every
deficiency of that kind. The weather being very
warm, would not admit of walking. We regaled
the family with a dish of tea at five o'clock. Took
a walk in the cool of the evening to the river. Re-
freshed ourselves with a porringer of pudding and
milk. Turned in between nine and ten, very sober.

Tuesday, June 25, 1776. I turned out at quarter
after four; cool, pleasant morning; being the first
up, saving our landlord and his son, who set out for
Providence early this morning, and by whom we
sent for some necessaries. I amused myself in walking about the farm until breakfast, which was coffee.
The weather growing very warm, we tarried in and
about the house during the heat of the day. Our

dinner consisted of salt pork and beef, and greens.
In the afternoon our landlady had a neighbor, a
woman, visiting. Drank tea, and towards evening
planted one hundred and twenty hills of beans,
which I brought from Newport. Mr. Nicoll set his
traps for squirrels, but without success, chatted until
after nine, drank our milk and retired to bed.

Wednesday, June 26, 1776. Turned out forty
minutes after four; pleasant morning; found our
landlord returned from Providence, but brings no
news; he brought us a loaf of sugar, a gallon of
rum, a few lemons, and some crackers; prices per
margin,[1] which is a specimen of the times. Our
breakfast, coffee. After breakfast Mr. Lechmere
and myself took a walk to the river, where Mr.
Nicoll was a fishing; he caught a few small fish.
It being very warm, we returned home at twelve
and had a bowl of punch. Our dinner provided was
fried pork and veal; we napped and chatted until
five o'clock, when we had a dish of green tea for the
first time, which was very agreeable; we diverted

1. In a marginal note in the manuscript Mr. Vernon gives the following
prices for these articles: Sugar per loaf, £2; rum per gallon, nine shillings;
lemons, nine pence each; crackers, one shilling per pound.

ourselves until evening, opened our bottle of olives, which was very good, and thanked the donor. Our landlord inclined much to talk of liberty and the times. We endeavored to waive the conversation. It is amazing what false and erroneous opinions and ideas these people have entertained, and what is worse, is that it is impossible for the human mind to undeceive them, such is their prejudice. We turned in about ten o'clock in good nature and spirits.

Thursday, June 27, 1776. Arose at five; pleasant, clear morning; wind at northeast. This day has been spent much like all the rest since we have been here, chiefly at home in idle chat, and now and then reading a page. Have not heard from home since we left; have been in great expectation of seeing Mr. A. Lechmere this day, but we are disappointed. We breakfasted on tea, and dined on veal and pork, cut small and put in the pot. The fields afforded us a fine sorrel for a salad, and Providence a good bowl of lemon punch. Nothing material this afternoon has happened, but I have the satisfaction in saying that a perfect harmony subsists between us and the family, but no neighbors' visits. Mr. Lechmere and I had three eggs each of us for our supper, which we procured from the neighbors. Turned in at ten; a very cool night.

Friday, June 28, 1776. Arose half after five; fine, clear, pleasant morning, which has been spent in chatting and cleaning ourselves, and delivering our foul linen to the house for washing. Our breakfast, coffee. Mr. Nicoll has been amusing himself this day in making a vane. Our seeds, before sown, are coming up, but the weather continues very dry as yet. Our landlord is preparing to go to a town meeting. I proposed to him that he would motion that we be sent for in order to give an account of ourselves, and that we be obliged to give security that we do not become a town charge, agreeably to a law of the Colony,[1] and in failure thereof to be ordered out of town. This conversation afforded us some amusement. Our dinner, pork, veal and greens, and a bowl of punch before dinner, after which we had a fine nap, and a dish of green tea

1. Acts and Laws of the English Colony of Rhode Island, Digest of 1767, p. 229.

at five P. M. We walked and talked until eight in the evening, when Mr. A. Lechmere made his appearance, a very welcome visitor, not having before the agreeable news of hearing from home. A bowl of punch being soon made, we remembered our Newport friends, chatted until after ten, and retired to bed quietly.

Saturday, June 29, 1776. Arose at ten minutes after five; pleasant morning, fresh breeze at about west. We chatted till breakfast, which was tea, after which we walked to the river, and A. Lechmere tried for trout but caught none, Mr. Nicoll took some pouts or toad fish; we returned at twelve, it being very warm. Made a cool bowl of punch, which was very refreshing. Dined upon a baked line of veal, part of a calf which was killed in the morning, with some sorrel for a salad. Took a nap after dinner and drank tea at five, watered our garden, etc., walked till our retirement. About eight o'clock Mr. Jabez Bowen,[1] of Providence, joined us. He

1. Jabez Bowen was born in Providence June 2, 1739. He was the son of Ephraim and Mary [Fenner] Bowen. He married Sarah, daughter of Obadiah Brown, December 19, 1762; second, Peddy Leonard, May 21, 1801. The first mention of Mr. Bowen in connection with Colonial business is with the

was very civil and entered on a conversation
[concerning] our banishment, and the cruel hard-
ship we sustained in consequence of the late act
of the Assembly. He pitied our fate, and offered
his services in assisting us all that lay in his power.
He is to see us again before he leaves the town.
We returned to the house about nine o'clock, drank
a porringer and turned in at ten, very sober.

development of the iron mine, discovered in 1765 on the north bank of the
Pawtuxet river. He was one of the founders of the Benevolent Congrega-
tional Society in 1771, and was for thirty years President of the Society. He
was a major and afterwards a colonel in the militia. An inspector of gun-
powder in 1775. Engaged in supplying cannon to the State in 1776. An
Associate Judge of the Superior Court from 1776 to 1779, and Chief Justice
of the same Court in 1781. A member of the Council of War in 1777-8, in
which body he did efficient service. In December, 1777, the Assembly, under
a recommendation of Congress, sent Mr. Bowen as one of her Commissioners
to attend a convention at New Haven. The business to be considered was the
regulation of the prices for labor, manufactures, internal produce and imported
goods (military stores excepted), and also the charges of Inn Holders. The
Commissioners were to report to the State Legislatures who were to pass laws.
Similar conventions were held on the same day at Fredericksburg, Va., and
Charleston, S. C. In 1778 Governor Bowen, in company with President James
Manning, were sent to Connecticut to obtain the repeal of the Land Embargo
Act. This act prevented the importation of grain into Rhode Island from that
State. The poor victims of the war were much in need of grain, and these
gentlemen were to obtain it. At the spring election of 1778 Mr. Bowen was
elected Deputy Governor, which office he held for three years. The British
were then in the possession of a large portion of Rhode Island. In all the
operations of the Continental forces, Governor Bowen was continually con-

Sunday, June 30, 1776. The bed being no longer agreeable I got up at half-past four. A very cloudy, disagreeable morning, but the sun soon dispelled the fog. Our landlord set out to visit his son at Kinnersly (Killingly), I amused myself in reading until breakfast, which was tea. It being very warm, we tarried in and about the house all the morning; made some punch at twelve, and dined upon part

sulted by Generals Spencer, Sullivan and Gates, successively. From 1781 to 1786 he was continued in the office of Deputy Governor. In the latter year the triumph of the Paper Money party overthrew the entire State government, and Governor Bowen with his party went out of power. The Tenth Bank, with all its infamous legislation, followed. In 1786 a convention was assembled at Annapolis to adopt some uniform system of commercial regulations. Out of this convention grew the Constitution of the United States. Governor Bowen was a delegate from Rhode Island, as he was also a member of the Rhode Island convention which adopted the Constitution, and voted for its adoption. He was appointed Loan Officer by Washington, and retained the office until the election of Jefferson. He was President of the Rhode Island Bible Society, and also President of the Rhode Island Agricultural Society. He assisted Benjamin West and Stephen Hopkins in their observations of the Transit of Venus in 1769, and he was a member of the first School Committee of the town of Providence in 1800. Governor Bowen was a graduate of Yale College. The degree of LL. D. was given him by Dartmouth. In 1785, upon the death of Stephen Hopkins, Governor Bowen was elected Chancellor of Rhode Island College, which office he retained until his death. This institution gave him the honorary degree of Master of Arts. He died at Providence, May 8, 1815, possessing to the last day of his life the highest respect and esteem of his fellow-men, and leaving a character of unsullied integrity.

2

of the calf's head, with a piece of pork and some
greens from the fields. The house affords us good
cider and good nature, two excellent ingredients for
the stomach and the mind. The latter being much
composed, we inclined to a nap. A very great appearance for rain in the afternoon, with some thunder,
but we are not blessed with any, which we greatly
lament. A dish of green tea pleased us much, and
in the cool of the evening took a walk. When we
returned, our girls were joined by a neighbor's daughter, which afforded us some innocent chat. At nine
I supped upon three eggs, and turned in before ten,
in tolerable good spirits.

Monday, July 1, 1776. Ten minutes before five
o'clock I turned out. This morning is very foggy
and disagreeable, which makes our people incline
for sleep. We amused ourselves in innocent chat
until breakfast, being coffee. We are much at a
loss, as the weather is bad, how to divert ourselves
this forenoon in the house. Mr. Nicoll, who is in-
defatigably industrious, is always proposing something to divert the mind, kept us constantly employed until dinner in some trifling matters. I

made some punch, after which we dined upon some stewed veal and pork. Soon after, Colonel Jabez Bowen called upon us to receive our commands, we commissioned him to procure us some necessaries from Providence. Mr. Nicoll and A. Lechmere tried for pickerel at King's Bridge,[1] but without success. Regaled ourselves and the family with a dish of tea, after which we assisted our friend Nicoll in putting up the vane at Nicoll Hall,[2] which we expect will be a matter of great speculation in the town. After we effected this business we returned to our lodgings, ate our milk and bread, and retired to bed between nine and ten.

Tuesday, July 2, 1776. Being the first up, as usual, just before five. Notwithstanding the weather is misty and wet, A. Lechmere mounted his horse about four o'clock for Newport. We each of us gave him a line to our wives for the first time. This day has been spent chiefly in the house on account of the badness of the weather. Our breakfast was

1. There were two bridges near Mr. Keach's house, both crossing the Chepachet river. It was probably one of these, then known by the name of King's Bridge, possibly the one nearest the pond now called Keach's Pond.

2. A nickname they had given to the barn.

coffee. Nothing very material occurred this fore-noon. I made some punch at twelve. Dined upon stewed veal and pork and greens. A little after two o'clock it began to thunder and rain, and so continued by showers till almost dark, when I pulled from our garden some lettuce and radishes, and some pepper grass, etc. Our supper was eggs and a drink of cyder. Turned in at half after nine.

Wednesday, July 3, 1776. Got up at a quarter after five. A very pleasant, clear, agreeable morn-ing. The wind about northwest. The rain, yester-day, has nourished the earth finely, and everything looks smiling and cheerful, which invited me to walk out before breakfast. Breakfast being coffee, after which Mr. Nicoll and myself went to work and put some green sods in the chimney in the hall, and gathered flowers from the fields and ornamented the same in the best manner we could, the first of the kind, I believe, were ever in this town. The heavens afforded us another small shower about eleven o'clock, which nourished the plants set out the day before. Treated ourselves with some punch, which whetted our appetites for the salt pork and greens. Afterwards we had a nap, and then played a game or two at whist, for want of a better employment. I then proposed a walk but they declined, saving Mr. Beale. We visited the mowers, our landlord and his two eldest sons having began this day—and very ordinary grass it is. This evening is the most remarkable cool that I ever knew in July. The wind continuing at northwest. I was very fearful there would be a frost in the night. Supped upon bread and milk, and turned in at a quarter-past nine.

Thursday, July 4, 1776. I arose at ten minutes after five o'clock. A very clear, cool morning. The wind still continuing at northwest. We tarried chiefly in the house this forenoon in shaving and cleaning ourselves. Our diversion was chiefly in innocent chat. We daily experience the good nature and civility of this family, which I cannot pass unnoticed. Our breakfast was coffee. We dined upon salt pork and greens, and a nap as usual; after we had drank a dish of tea, we walked out and assisted our landlord and his sons in raking hay until evening. Having purchased a lamb of Mr. Keetch (Keach) for our table, Mr. Beale saw it dressed. It is a tolerably good one. Our supper was a few eggs, boiled, and milk. Went to bed at half after nine.

Friday, July 5, 1776. Being more sleepy than usual I did not get up until ten minutes before six. The wind at southwest, cloudy, and almost calm, but as the sun grew higher the wind increased. We spent this day in and about the house. I amused myself in whittling a walking stick. At twelve o'clock we used the last lemon, and were not forgetful of our Newport friends. Dined half after twelve upon the forequarter of the lamb purchased yesterday, roasted, and the head pry'd with mint, and a sorrel salad. At two o'clock a small shower of rain. The wind still continuing very windy and cloudy. Half after five very considerable (to use the term of the country) showers of rain until almost sun setting, attended with thunder and sharp lightning and some hail. In the evening we all took a walk out, it being very pleasant, and soon after returned. Joseph, the boy of the house, by some accident cut his foot with the drawing knife, very badly; it bled much. Mr. Lechmere's Turlington[1] was very useful on this occasion. Our supper consisted of bread and milk. Turned in at half after nine.

Saturday, July 6, 1776. I arose at ten minutes before five. A clear, calm morning. The wind about northwest. The weather, I think, very cool for the season; it continued so all the forenoon. Our time before breakfast (being coffee) was employed in cleaning our shoes, shaving, etc. The whole forenoon has been spent chiefly in the house in chatting with the girls. We lament greatly the want of books to amuse us, which we have neglected. Stephen, our landlord's eldest son, told us that he is a member of a company at Scituate, who some time past, have collected some money which they have laid out in books, to be loaned out to the company. It is called the Scituate Library.[2] Our landlord

1. This word is probably a corruption of Tourniquet, brought about by an error in transcribing or misspelling.

2. Mr. Wilkinson, in his Genealogy of the Wilkinson Family, relates of this Library that it was established at a very early period at, or near the residence of Captain Samuel Wilkinson, the grandfather of Stephen Hopkins. The residence of Mr. Wilkinson is given as having been in that part of Providence since called Smithfield. Mr. Wilkinson does not say near the residence of the late Captain Samuel Wilkinson, or that the former residence, etc.,—but it is near his residence,—this leads to the inference that Captain Wilkinson

attended the funeral of a young man who died suddenly. The procession passed by our house at one o'clock to the Baptist meeting-house, where is to be a sermon on the occasion. Esquire Wilmut (Wilmarth) called in to see us for the first time, with whom we had conversation respecting our sufferings; he tarried with us about half an hour, and promised to see us again soon. I made a bowl of currant punch. Dined upon stewed veal and pork, with a sorrel salad. The weather growing very warm induced me to take a nap in the chair, which was very refreshing. We received a small keg of biscuit from Colonel Bowen. Took a walk in the fields at six to visit the haymakers. The wind all this day con-

---

was still living and that the Library was established before August, 1727, which was the time of Captain Wilkinson's death. But Scituate was not known at that period. In 1730–1 the three towns of Scituate, Smithfield and Glocester were incorporated, so that it is not probable that the Library was established before the latter date. It may, however, be considered certain that this Public Library was among the earliest, if not the earliest, in Rhode Island. In these early years there came from this region very well educated, and very able men; may we not reasonably infer that it was from this source that their learning came? They had not schools, they must have read these books, and thinking did the rest.

The house of the late Elisha Mathewson in Scituate, where this library remained, was recently burned and the old library was thus destroyed.

tinues northerly; our supper, milk and bread, and as usual went to bed at half after nine.

Sunday, July 7, 1776. Arose just at five o'clock; cloudy morning, little wind, easterly but got to the southwest about noon; a clear sky the middle of the afternoon. At six o'clock our landlord's two daughters, with Jeremiah, set out for Kinersly (Killingly) meeting and returned in the evening. We tarried in the house all day, till towards sun setting. At twelve Mr. Nicoll made some small toddy. Dined upon boiled lamb, pork and greens. Took a small nap in the chair, and diverted myself with a book until half after four, when our landlord returned from meeting and brought with him Esquires Brown and Wilmut (Wilmarth), the latter with his lady, whom we received kindly; they tarried after six; we took a walk in the fields after tea. Upon our return, just before the setting of the sun, we discovered six men on horseback, and soon after nine or ten more horses. The first division rode very fierce up to the house and alighted from their horses, came into the house where Mr. Keetch (Keach) was and asked some questions respecting us. The others continued on horseback. Three ladies were on single horses and two double, that is to say, a man and woman. We desired them to light and walk in, but they refused excepting one young man, who came into our room, but said nothing. After they had satisfied their curiosity by looking and staring at the Tories, they paraded about on their horses for some time before the house and went off. In some places they would be called young bricks; they were very wild and awkward in their behavior. We supped on a few eggs boiled, and chatted till almost ten when we went to bed.

Monday, July 8, 1776. Arose before five; a very clear morning; the wind northwest. This forenoon has been spent in and about the house, having shaved and cleaned ourselves. Breakfast, coffee, but Mr. Beale always prefers milk. Made a little weak toddy before dinner, which was a roasted quarter of lamb, with sorrel for a salad. The afternoon growing very warm, inclined to a nap in the chair. Took a small walk in the evening, eat our bread and milk, and retired to bed a quarter before ten.

Tuesday, July 9, 1776. Arose a quarter before

six; a very clear, calm morning; what little air
there is seems to be northerly. I find that our vane,
which was put up some days ago upon the barn, is
taken down by some person or persons, which I am
sorry for, as it deprives us of the pleasure of knowing where the wind blows, but if it gives umbrage
am content. Our breakfast was coffee, soon after
which, about fifteen or twenty rods northwest from the
house, we discovered a fox. The dog pursued him
in the woods for some time, but without success.
We sauntered about the house until twelve o'clock
when we had a drink of toddy. Our dinner was a
cold lamb pie, had a short nap afterwards; chatted
a while and then adjourned to the hall, where we
had a pool at quadrille. Took a walk in the cool of
the evening. Our supper was a few boiled eggs.
Retired to bed before ten.

Wednesday, July 10, 1776. Arose about five;
cloudy, calm morning. Our landlord set out for
Providence; we desired the favor of him that he
would take a letter from us to Secretary Henry
Ward, unsealed, which we read to him. He absolutely refused taking it. So that we are deprived

of the benefit of remonstrating our unhappy situation. About seven discovered, we think, the same red fox chasing the fowls, about ten or fifteen rods north from the house, but he soon made to the woods. Our breakfast, coffee. We stayed in the house this forenoon. A drink of toddy at twelve. Our dinner consisted of the remainder of the cold lamb pie, boiled pork, beef and greens. About two o'clock it began to thunder and rain, which continued for an hour and a half, when it cleared away finely. We had a pool at quadrille at the hall, and a walk to Prospect Hill in the evening. Our supper, bread and milk. Between nine and ten our landlord returned from Providence. He showed us an order from Governor Cooke, directed to the Sheriff of the County of Providence, to remove us to some other house in the town of Glocester. He saw my brother Will at Secretary Ward's office, but he did not think it proper to ask after me. We turned in about ten o'clock.

Thursday, July 11, 1776. Arose a few minutes after five; a very pleasant, clear, calm morning; before seven it became cloudy and thick, the wind easterly, so that it was necessary for us to keep the house. We diverted ourselves with the girls and the family. They are very chatty respecting our departure and destination. Before twelve o'clock it began to rain, and continued till two. Our dinner consisted of cold lamb pie, bread and cheese. Before three it cleared up finely, between five and six were very agreeable showers, and before sun setting it cleared up again, with a fine rainbow in the southeast and the wind southwest. In the evening it was remarkably cool, walked to Prospect Hill. The wind changed before bed-time to northwest. The Count and myself supped upon eggs, and chatted till between nine and ten, and went to bed.

Friday, July 12, 1776. Arose a few minutes before five ; a very fine, clear, calm morning. I should imagine by the coolness of the air that there must have been a frost in the neighborhood in the night. Landlord and his wife set out at seven for Chestnut Hill[1] to meeting, about nine miles distant, where was a baptizing of four persons. The religion of

1. Chestnut Hill is a village in the town of Killingly, Connecticut, situated but a short distance from the line which separates the two States.

3

the people of this town consists entirely of New Light Baptists. The custom of Dipping is much in vogue in this and the neighboring towns. Our breakfast was coffee, as usual. We diverted ourselves in the house this forenoon. Our dinner consisted of a boiled cheek and greens, with an Indian pudding; had a short nap in the chair. Mr. Nicoll took a long walk, and visited some of the neighbors. The others of our company assisted in getting up the hay, after which we walked to Prospect Hill. The weather is still very cool, the wind about west. Our supper, milk and bread; turned in between nine and ten.

Saturday, July 13, 1776. Got up a few minutes before five; cloudy morning, and still very cool, wind easterly. The last night was taken down by some persons the staff on the barn which our vane was fixed upon. Reynard made his appearance again about seven o'clock within a hundred yards of the door after the fowls; the dog pursued him but in vain. Our breakfast, coffee. Mr. Nicoll ventured to take a long walk westward; we diverted ourselves in the best manner we could in the house, the females especially being very sociable and obliging to us. Our dinner, pork, beef and greens. The weather being dull and cloudy we courted a nap in the chair. About five o'clock a walk was proposed to the river, where we washed our feet. On our way home we spied a striped squirrel which we chased from one stone heap to another and at last lost him, which much grieved Mr. Nicoll, as he has a fondness for getting one of these animals. On our return to the house we found Miss Fenner,[1] a very likely, tall, agreeable young lady, about seventeen or eighteen. She brought us a packet of letters from our families, long wished for. You may think it was a cordial to us, not having heard from home for two weeks. Miss Fenner tarried with us an hour, and promised to see us again soon and drink tea. The letters were delivered to her by Mr. Callender at Smithfield. Our supper, pudding and milk. Went to bed before ten, in good humor and spirits. I forgot to mention that General West passed by the house this morning about eight o'clock and saluted us. I

1. Frequent mention is made in the Diary of Mr. Fenner, and of his daughter. John Fenner, a prominent citizen of the town, is doubtless meant. There were many families in the adjoining town of Johnston by this name.

proposed to bring him to, and require of him the
countersign; if refused, to detain him at headquarters.

Sunday, July 14, 1776. Arose eight minutes before five; very calm, dull, cloudy morning. It
began to rain moderately at seven o'clock. Our
breakfast, coffee with Jonny[1] cake buttered. The
family not being disposed for meeting, saving the
landlord and Christopher, we spent the day in reading and innocent chat, our two young ladies contributing much to our happiness. Dinner, salt pork,
with dried corn and beans. The Count[2]—am fearful
is not very well, as he cannot eat his allowance,
though he generally takes his share of cider and
a quart to three pints of milk morning and evening.
A nap was agreeable this dull day. Christopher
informs us that a Liberty Pole is erected nigh Elder
Winsor's[3] meeting house, with a weather vane and

1. The spelling here of the word Jonny is the same which Mr. Thomas R.
Hazard (Shepherd Tom) contended in his recent papers, published in the
Providence Journal, was the only correct way. It seems to be an authority for
Mr. Hazard.

2. A nickname given to Mr. Lechmere.

3. Elder Samuel Winsor's Meeting House was in the town of Johnston. It
was built in 1774. The congregation were Six Principle Baptists. They

our staff and spindle. It ceased raining before sun-
setting, and we had a small walk. Our supper was
pudding and milk. Turned in half after nine, as
usual.

Monday, July 15, 1776. Arose at twenty minutes
before six. Thick, cloudy morning, with small rain,
cleared up before eleven o'clock; a fine day. Our
breakfast, coffee. We diverted ourselves in the
house till dinner, it being the remainder of the cold
pork and beans of yesterday, warmed up. A small
nap in the chair; at five a pool at Quadrille[1] in the
hall, and a walk upon the hill, where we met with
Mr. Burr,[2] the Deputy Sheriff of Providence, who
informed us that the Governor had called the Assembly to meet on Thursday next at Newport.

separated from the church in Providence on a question of Doctrine, "some
holding to commune with those that were not under hands, and others not."
Elder Winsor died in January, 1802. (Knight's Hist. Six Prin. Bap., p. 282.)

1. Quadrille is a game at cards played by four persons. The four tens,
nines and eights are discarded from the pack. There is a pool in which the
players deposit or withdraw whatever stake is played for. When three persons
play the game, it was known as Ombre; both terms are used in the Diary, see
July 20. It is the game celebrated by Pope in the Rape of the Lock, Canto iii.

2. David Burr was keeper of His Majesty's Jail in Providence in 1765; at a
later period he was a Deputy from North Providence. He was doubtless the
person here referred to.

Whereupon we held a consultation on the subject of applying for our relief. Our supper, milk and bread; retired to bed at ten.

Tuesday, July 16, 1776. Arose half after four; a clear morning but very cold; wrote letters to Henry Ward[1] and James Honyman,[2] Esquires, to

1. This gentleman was the son of Governor Richard Ward, and a brother of Samuel and Thomas Ward. He was Secretary of State for thirty-seven years, from 1760 to 1797. This latter year the period of his death. His father had been Secretary, as also his brother Thomas, who, dying in 1760, while in office, was succeeded by Henry. These three members of one family had held the office of Secretary of State upwards of seventy years. A sister of Mr. Ward's, Miss Amey, married Samuel Vernon, a brother of our Diarist, and a very prominent merchant of Newport. Mr. Ward was an earnest supporter of the Revolution, and was entrusted by his contemporaries with every species of public trust. Upon the passage of the act suspending Governor Wanton from performing the functions of his office, and until the Deputy Governor, Cooke, was formally invested with authority, the entire Executive authority was devolved by the Assembly upon Mr. Ward. He died November 25, 1797.

2. James Honyman, Esq., was the son of the Rev. James Honyman, rector of Trinity Church, Newport, and Missionary sent from England by the Society for the Propagation of the Gospel in Foreign Parts. Little is known of the birth or education of the son. He was made Attorney General of the Colony in 1732, and held the office until 1741. He was a member of the commission to settle the boundary dispute between Massachusetts and Rhode Island in 1741. In 1756 he was elected Senator and annually until 1764. In 1755 he was one of a commission appointed to attend the Congress called by the Earl of Loudoun. He received from the Crown the appointment of Advocate General to the Court of Vice Admiralty in the Colony. This office he held until 1776, when the rupture between the Colonies and the Mother Country rendered his position

solicit our removal, by way of Petition to the General Assembly. Also wrote letter to Captain Handy,[1] which our landlord was kind enough to carry to Providence, for which place he started at half after eleven. Our breakfast, coffee. We tarried in and about the house this forenoon, and spread some hay which was in the barn. Our dinner consisted of salt pork, beef and greens. Soon after turned the hay. A small pool at Quadrille, then put the above

a most uncomfortable one to occupy. Thereupon he went to the Assembly and stated his wish to resign his commission if desired by the Assembly. The Assembly passed a vote stating that his holding it was disagreeable to them, and requesting him to surrender it into the possession of the Sheriff—to be by him deposited with the Secretary. Mr. Honyman died (January or February) 15, 1778, aged sixty-seven years, a most worthy gentleman. Mr. Updike relates that most of the daughters and grand-daughters of Mr. Honyman married British officers or Americans adhering to the Crown, and departed with the enemy, leaving no lineal descendents here.

1. Possibly Charles Handy, one of Mr. Vernon's subscribers to the Boston Chronicle. The Boston Chronicle, a newspaper published under the auspices of the English authorities, was bitterly hostile to the Colonists. So exasperating to them was this paper that in 1770 John Mein, one of its editors, was obliged to leave the country and return to England. Mr. Vernon, in his capacity as Postmaster, acted as agent for this paper and obtained in Newport many subscribers. The list of his subscribers for 1767 has recently been printed in the Newport Historical Magazine, with a note from James E. Mauran, Esq., from which the preceding facts are taken. This list discloses the names as subscribers of the party banished with Mr. Vernon, and also several of those subsequently banished or otherwise dealt with by the Assembly.

hay into cocks. Drank tea. About seven o'clock
A. Lechmere[1] and Silas Cooke[2] arrived from Newport, chatted some time, eat our milk and bread,
and went to bed at ten o'clock. This afternoon a
very fresh breeze at the southwest, but little sun,
began to rain at nine o'clock.

Wednesday, July 17, 1776. Arose eight minutes
before five; fine morning, little wind; our landlord
arrived [last evening] from Providence after we
were in bed. He brought a letter from Mr. Ward,
but no encouragement for our release. He brought
us a gallon of rum. Our breakfast, coffee. Messrs.
Lechmere and Cooke left us to go home at twenty
minutes after nine. We walked up the hills southward, and then returned home where we tarried till

1. Anthony Lechmere was probably a brother of Nicholas. By the act of
July, 1776, banishing eleven persons, Anthony Lechmere was banished to
Glocester, where his brother then was. When, at the next Assembly, the
Sheriff made his return, it appears that Mr. Lechmere was not to be found, he
having embarked on board a vessel belonging to William Vernon and sailed
for the West Indies.

2. Silas Cooke, Jun., was one of the eleven persons banished by the act of
July, 1776. Mr. Cooke was sent to South Kingstown. At the September session
the Assembly voted that Mr. Cooke be allowed to remove himself into the
town of Middletown, on Rhode Island, he confining himself to said town until
further orders.

dinner, which consisted of stewed veal and pork. The weather being very pleasant and warm induced us to take a nap. Mr. Nicoll's son Charles came to us while at dinner, having walked from Providence. We spent our time for the most part in the house until tea, when we took a walk to the southward. Mr. Nicoll and Charles went a fishing, and caught a few toad fish.[1] Our girls have been a visiting their sister all day. Freelove, only, returned in the even-ing. Our people from mowing brought home a black snake upwards of four feet long, which they had killed. Our supper, milk and bread. Turned in at half after nine. Wind this day north, north-west and northwest.

Thursday, July 18, 1776. Arose twenty minutes after five ; calm, pleasant morning, but the sun soon shot in. Mr. Lechmere turned out of bed about six, which I can't help noticing. We generally breakfast at seven or before, and that upon coffee, saving Mr. Beale, who chooses milk. Mr. Beale and I walked

---

1. There is a fish called properly a Toad Fish, but it is not that which is here referred to. In another entry, June 29, Mr. Vernon speaks of Toad Fish or pouts. Doubtless he meant the fish known now as horned pouts or bull-heads.

to the northward this forenoon, where we saw four females pulling flax, a circumstance we can't help remarking, as it is the first of the kind we have seen.[1] This we imagine is owing to the scarcity of hands at this time [of the year]. Our dinner consisted of baked veal, with a small piece of pork, and that commonly at twelve, and a small nap afterwards. We kept in and about the house till about four, when we had a pool at Quadrille at Nicoll Hall, afterwards took a walk, although it looked much like rain. The wind being at the southeast, about right. Our Patty got home from her visit. Our supper, milk and bread. Turned in at nine o'clock.

Friday, July 19, 1776. Arose twenty-five minutes after five o'clock. In the night it thundered and lightened, with rain. This morning a very fresh breeze, about south. The weather squally and unsettled. We gathered a mess of peas, the first and the last that we are likely to have this season. We

---

1. The meaning is here ambiguous. But by the term scarcity of hands the inference is that these were the first women laboring in the fields which they had seen, and they noted the fact. The pulling of flax must have been common to them, for the State had for many years paid heavy bounties, and large amounts of it had been raised. Rhode Island had at this time five regiments in service. Hence the scarcity of men.

picked also some beans, both of which we had for dinner, with a boiled leg of veal and pork, and we eat heartily. The weather cleared up very finely between twelve and one o'clock, and was quite warm, which invited us to take a nap. The whole family being pleasant and good natured, we treated them to a dish of tea, the first trial of that which was sent to me by Mrs. Vernon. It was much liked. Mr. Beale and myself took a long walk. The evening being vastly agreeable, we had the pleasure of seeing the moon, being the first time since her change. Our supper, milk and bread; retired to bed before ten.

Saturday, July 20, 1776. Arose twenty minutes after five; a very fine, calm, serene, pleasant morning. A very great dew in the night. Our breakfast, coffee. Took a walk out and amused myself in the house the remainder of the forenoon. Mr. Fenner sent our landlord a hind quarter of good veal, part of the leg we had fried for dinner, with some pork, and a short nap afterwards. We tarried till four o'clock in and about the house, when we

played a while at Ombre[1] in the hall, and then Mr.
Beale and I took a walk south and north of our dis-
trict; in our ramble I killed a Thract (Thrush) with
a stone. I brought it home. There has been little
wind all day from west to west northwest. Our
supper, milk and bread. Went to bed at a quarter
after nine.

Sunday, July 21, 1776. Arose twenty minutes
before five. This morning little wind, cloudy, appearance of rain. Our breakfast, coffee. This forenoon we shaved and cleaned ourselves. Most of the
family are preparing for meeting. Our dinner, baked
line of veal, with sorrel salad and peppergrass of our
sowing. A nap ensued. Our family brought home
their daughter, Winsor, after meeting, and we all
drank tea together; an agreeable, sociable woman
she is, a virtue the other sex does not seem to be
endued with. We had a long walk after tea. Our
supper, bread and milk. It began to rain between
eight and nine o'clock, and continued until half-past
nine, when we went to bed.

Monday, July 22, 1776. Arose five minutes after

1. See note concerning Quadrille on page 29.

five. Pleasant, fine morning. Breakfast, coffee.
We spent the forepart of this day chiefly in the
house in making a snuff mill, our snuff being almost expended. Dinner, boiled leg of veal and
pork, with some greens. After chatting a while had
a small nap, and a pool at Quadrille in the hall, a
dish of tea, and a walk this afternoon; small wind,
southerly, and most remarkably warm. We pulled
some radishes from our own seed, which were tolerably good. I can't help observing that not one of the
family ever tasted or saw one before, but they liked
them much. Milk and bread for supper, and to bed
half after nine.

Tuesday, July 23, 1776. Arose half after five;
cloudy morning, with a little wind, easterly; breakfast, coffee. The Count is something better this day.
Yesterday he complained of a fever, but we observed
that he ate his allowance very well. His disorder,
upon examination, proved to be the Turkey Fever,[1]
the effects of good cider. Rain began to fall at half
after nine, showers all the forepart of the day. Our

---

1. What this means is incomprehensible to the editor.

4

dinner a gammon,[1] with peas and beans from our garden, and a nap. Cleared up in the afternoon. Played a hand at quadrille. Before tea took a long walk with Mr. Beale. Our supper, pudding and milk; retired to bed at a quarter after nine.

Wednesday, July 24, 1776. Arose at a quarter after five. A very thick, foggy morning, but cleared away before breakfast. For breakfast we had coffee. One of our neighbors sent us a side of pretty good lamb at 30 ——. Fried the loin with some pork for dinner, and after it a nap. We tarried in the house all the afternoon, the weather being thick and not agreeable. Drank a dish of tea with the family, and afterwards took a very considerable walk with Mr. Beale. The wind southerly. Supped upon milk and bread, and went to bed at half after nine.

Thursday, July 25, 1776. Arose at a quarter before six. The morning being very thick and cloudy. The wind northwest. The sun appeared before breakfast. For breakfast we had coffee. We amused ourselves in making snuff with the new mill until dinner. For dinner we had a leg of lamb, with

1. A gammon is a smoked ham.

pork boiled with greens, and young turnips. At one
o'clock Mr. T. Wyatt[1] came to visit us from Newport. He brought some necessaries and the pleasing
news that our families were well. He tarried with
us till nigh six o'clock, when he started on his return. This is called a very warm day. We visited
the Hall,[2] and assisted our landlord in getting up his
hay till after dark. Supped on milk and bread. A
remarkably fine, bright evening. Retired to bed at
a quarter before ten o'clock.

Friday, July 26, 1776. Arose at a quarter after
five o'clock; a very fine, clear morning. Our breakfast, coffee, with radishes, after which the wind began
to breeze up, though light, at about northwest. The
weather now becomes warm, which obliges us to keep
house more than we would choose. We had a forequarter of lamb roasted for dinner, and a boiled

1. This may possibly be an error in transcribing; the T may have been
intended for J. James Wyatt was a royalist. He left Rhode Island and fled
to New York, where, in 1780, his wife, Mrs. Elizabeth Wyatt, joined him,
having first sought and obtained permission of the Assembly. She carried her
two children, a servant, and her household furniture. In the entry of August
25, and subsequent dates, the name of Mr. Wyatt is clearly written out James.
These were without doubt the same individual.

2. Nicoll Hall, otherwise the barn.

smoked cheek, with beans of two kinds, and peas, the fruits of Newport. Our landlady and the two young ladies dined with us for the first time, in the parlor. Mr. Beale exerted himself in the cooking with great applause, and we dined heartily. Delivered a shirt or two to the house for washing, and adjourned to the easterly part of the house for coolness. About four o'clock we were agreeably surprised by the arrival of W. Bardin[1] and Mrs. Wright.[2] We enjoyed their company and drank tea, till about six o'clock when they took leave of us for Esquire Williams's,[3] though we walked about a mile [with them] and am in hopes of seeing them again before they leave the town. Mrs. Vernon was so kind as to compliment me with a new shirt, and the Count's lady was not unmindful of him, which we thankfully partake of. Oh the excellency of

1. William Bardin, a resident of Newport, was the father-in-law of Mr. Vernon. Mrs. Mary Mears, a widow, and a daughter of Mr. Bardin, became Mr. Thomas Vernon's second wife.

2. Possibly the wife of Benjamin Wright, one of Mr. Vernon's subscribers to the Boston Chronicle.

3. Silas Williams, Esq., at that time one of the Representatives from the town of Glocester to the Assembly. His house was three-quarters of an hour's walk from Mr. Keach's house. See entry, August 24.

bread and milk, the effect of which is agreeable sleep and pleasing dreams. We retired at half after nine.

Saturday, July 27, 1776. Arose twenty minutes before five. The morning is clear and pleasant. Our breakfast, coffee. About half after nine W. Bardin made us a visit from Esquire Williams's, and dined with us on a shoulder of lamb and boiled pork with beans. He tarried with us till after three o'clock. We walked with him [on his return] as far as was convenient, when we returned and played at Quadrille. Took a small walk to the northward. Eat our bread and milk, and went to bed at a quarter after nine. The wind easterly the whole day. N. B.—No bedbugs, and the first flea saw this morning since we have been here.

Sunday, July 28, 1776. Arose ten minutes before six. Mr. Beale was first up. His second time since we left Newport. The weather cloudy and little wind. The wind breezed up at about nine o'clock from the southeast. Shirted, shaved, and cleaned ourselves; spent some time in reading both before and after dinner. For dinner we had a boiled tongue from Newport, a piece of pork, some French turnips and some carrots. Drank tea, with radishes, after our people returned from meeting. Took a walk in a circle of three miles. Eat our milk and bread. After supper our landlord informed us that the town was very uneasy at our stay here, and expressed his desire of our being removed to some other house, for it was no longer convenient for his family to entertain us, and that he must think of some method for our removal. Our conversation lasted till eleven o'clock, when we went to bed.

Monday, July 29, 1776. Arose at six o'clock; a very rainy morning. The wind about south. Breakfast, coffee, with radishes. We had some conversation with our landlord relative to our removal, but nothing decisive. Mr. Charles Nicoll went off to Newport at eleven o'clock. Our dinner was a small piece of our cold tongue, and pork with dried corn and beans. This has been a very dull, melancholy day. The weather squally with showers of rain. The wind from southeast to south. A man of the town brought a hind quarter of veal to the house, which we purchased at six shillings, old tenor, per pound. The badness of the weather confined us to the house all day, which is tedious. Our supper, milk and bread. Went to bed half after nine.

Tuesday, July 30, 1776. Arose exactly at six o'clock. The wind northerly, and an appearance of fair weather. It rained very hard in the night, attended with heavy thunder and sharp lightning. Our breakfast, tea, with Jonny cake and radishes. By leave of our landlady, we picked some beans and the remainder of the peas in the garden, which we had for dinner, with a loin of veal, baked. We have discovered for some days past a very great coolness and indifferency towards us in the family. This behavior gives us great uneasiness, as we are conscious that we have given no just cause for their being offended. We tarried in the house till after three o'clock. It being very warm, we adjourned to the Hall, it being a cool situation, and diverted ourselves with a pool at Quadrille. Afterwards Mr. Nicoll, Mr. Beale and myself, took a walk and killed a snake in the way. The sky being very clear, we had an opportunity of viewing the eclipse of the

moon[1] very-distinctly. As usual, our supper of milk
and bread; retired to bed half after nine.

Wednesday, July 31, 1776. Arose ten minutes
before five. A very clear, calm, fine morning. A
great dew last night. We had radishes with our
tea for breakfast. Afterwards walked down to the
river. Delivered our foul linen to S. Keach's wife
to be washed. Washed our feet and returned home
to dinner; it consisted of fried veal, pork and
cucumbers. Tarried at home till after three, and
then went to the Hall, played at Quadrille a while.
Went in the woods and gathered some ——. Afterwards we all took a walk to the northward.
Can't help noticing that the farmers in the town are
much backward in their work. The grass and grain
suffer greatly for not being cut in season, and the
corn for not being hoed. The reason is plain that
there are not people left to do the necessary work.[2]

1. Benjamin West, the Rhode Island astronomer, gives, in his Almanac for
1776, a minute account of this total eclipse of the moon. The duration of
the eclipse was 3 h. 30 m. 48 sec. The duration of total darkness was
1 h. 32 m. 38 sec.

2. The exigencies of the military service had drawn heavily upon Rhode
Island. She had at this time five regiments in the field. Three in the Continental service and two within the State.

Eat our pudding and milk. Mr. Beale always turns
in at nine o'clock. Mr. Nicoll uncertain, and the
Count and I generally at half after nine. The wind
before sunset got to southeast and breezed up. This
may be called a warm day.

Thursday, August 1, 1776. This morning I arose
just at six o'clock. The weather somewhat cloudy ;
little wind, southerly. The sun appeared about
eight. Our breakfast, tea, with radishes. It is remarkable that we had this vegetable large in size in
three weeks after sowing the seed. This forenoon
has been spent in the house, being attentive to our
little affairs, shaving, shirting, etc. Our dinner was
the remainder of the leg of veal, with pork, French
turnips and cucumbers. The weather for the most
part of the day was cloudy, windy, and sultry. A
short nap in the chair was agreeable. About three
o'clock Mr. Beale and myself took a walk in the
woods, and picked some W. [whortle] Berries. Mr.
Nicoll and the Count walked separately, but missed
of us. But we all met at the Hall at five, and played
at Quadrille till seven, when we all took a small walk
southerly. My supper, W. Berries [whortleberries]

and milk. Chatted till half after nine and retired to bed. N. B.—A meeting was to have been at neighbor Johnson's this afternoon, but as no person was there but Mr. Nicoll, the man of the house prayed and he was dismissed. The religious people of this town call themselves New Light[1] Baptists. Preachers and exhorters are innumerable. Any one gifted in this way commands their respect, and are styled Elders.

Friday, August 2, 1776. I arose twenty-five minutes after five. The morning is cloudy, with little wind, westerly. It continued so all the morning, which induced us to keep in the house. By leave of our landlady we gathered some beans, which we had for dinner, with salt pork, a piece of salt beef, and a W. Berry pudding. In the afternoon the sun ap-

1. The New Light Baptists arose from the revival which succeeded the advent of Whitefield in New England in 1740. The movement was in derision called the New Light stir. The work began among the Pedobaptists (or those who believe in infant baptism),—where there was opposition a separation took place—hence the term Separates, as applied to some churches. These people were highly evangelical, and held clear and consistent views of religious discipline. Their creed was the Bible. They did not consider education to be a necessary qualification for a clergyman, but they permitted anyone who felt moved by the Spirit to become an exhorter. Few, if any, of these Separate churches remain distinct from the Baptist denomination at the present time.

peared, and it was warm. We played a pool at
Quadrille in the Hall. About five the wind shifted
to the northwest, which made the air much cooler.
At six Mr. Beale and myself took a walk of three
miles circle. The other gentlemen chose to keep at
home, where we joined them in the evening; eat
our milk and bread, chatted till half after nine, and
went to bed.

Saturday, August 3, 1776. Arose after five. The
weather is clear and pleasant, but rather cool; a
small air of wind, northerly. Mr. Beale usually rises
about six, Mr. Nicoll about seven, Mr. Lechmere
at eight, sometimes before and sometimes after.
Our breakfast, tea, with radishes. I diverted myself this day in finishing a powder horn for Mr.
Nicoll. Our dinner, a Gammon, boiled, with cucumbers and a sorrel salad. I must remark that there
lives about a quarter of a mile from our house an
old man of eighty years of age. He says his name
is —— Johnson; he was born in London and came
a passenger with above sixty others (I imagine
for the better peopling of that country). His mind
is much poisoned with the disorder of the country.

He is a very great Politician, and he walks to our house (though very poorly) almost every day, and sometimes twice a day, in order to read the Providence newspaper and paraphrase upon it. He says he was on board of Captain Elliott's [sloop] in the famous engagement with the Pirate nigh Block Island. He gave us a particular[1] account of the

1. This memorandum concerning the capture and trial of the Pirates is so confused that it is impossible to understand it. It is here given, it is true, as the random recollection of a man upwards of eighty years of age, and related upwards of a half century after the event. Mr. Henry Bull, in his Memoirs of Rhode Island, has given a concise history of the affair. His note has been reproduced by Mr. Updike in his Memoirs of the Rhode Island Bar. Mr. Updike also reprinted in this book the very rare account of the Trial, which was printed at the time. Mr. Bull's note runs thus: "Two Pirate sloops, the Ranger and the Fortune, which had committed various piracies on the high seas, being in company, on the 8th of May, 1723, captured the ship 'Amsterdam Merchant,' John Welland, master, the day after which capture they plundered and sunk the ship. On the 6th of June, in latitude 39 (Block Island is in latitude 42) they took a Virginia sloop, rifled her, and let her go. The following day this Virginia sloop fell in with His Majesty's ship Grey Hound, twenty guns, Captain Solgard, commander, and related the circumstances of their capture and release. Captain Solgard sailed immediately in pursuit, and on the 10th came up with the Pirate sloops about fourteen leagues south of the eastern end of Long Island. They, mistaking the Grey Hound for a merchant ship, gave chase and soon commenced firing on her, under a black flag; they soon hauled down the black flag and hoisted a red flag. The Grey Hound succeeded in capturing one of the sloops, after having seven men wounded. The other sloop escaped. The Grey Hound came with the prize into the harbor of Newport, and the pirates, thirty-six in number, were

battle, and of the conduct of the commanders of
the two sloops. Elliott was the greatest pol-
troon and coward that he ever saw or heard
of. Captain Clarke behaved something better.
In short, in describing the behavior and manner

committed for trial. The trial followed on the 10th of July and the following
days. Twenty-six were sentenced to be hanged. The execution took place on
Gravelly Beach, on the 19th July, 1723. The bodies were buried on Goat or
Fort Island, between high and low water mark." Some additional notes are
needed to render this account quite complete. There is a discrepancy between
the number of men convicted and sentenced to be hanged as stated in the
Trial, and the list of names of the men actually hanged. The first account
numbers twenty-eight, and the last twenty-six. The names of two men who were
convicted and sentenced, viz., John Brown and Patrick Cunningham. There
were two men named John Brown; they were denominated "the shortest" and
"the tallest"; both were sentenced to be hanged. Thus it appears twenty-eight
were hanged instead of twenty-six. This error in numbers has crept into all
Rhode Island histories. The sloop captured was the Ranger, commanded by
Captain Edward Low. The sloop which escaped was the "Fortune," commanded by Captain Lowther. Captain Low had the *good fortune* to be at the
time of the action on board of the "Fortune" and thus escaped capture. From
one of the old Colony cash books may be gathered some curious memoranda
connected with this event :

Sheriff Brenton, for Executing the Pyrates,	£138 2 0
Richard Clark, for Account of the Pyrates,	64 1 1
John Harris, for looking after ye wounded Pyrates,	30 0 0
James Jackson, for dinners for ye Judges of ye Pyrates,	22 8 0
John Valentine, for order of ye Pyrates,	10 0 0
Daniel Updike, for order of ye Pyrates,	5 0 0

This Court was composed of the Governor of Massachusetts, the Governor
of Rhode Island, four Members of the Massachusetts Council, and the Sur-

5

of the father, he pictured the son in very lively colors.[1] We tarried in the house till after tea, when we all went to the river at Sil Keach's[2] for our clean linen. The people are poor, with many children, and the woman is thankful for this job. We returned home in the evening, eat our supper of milk and bread, and to bed at twenty minutes after nine. The weather is cool in the evening.

Sunday, August 4, 1776. Arose a minute before

veyor-General of North America. This singular composition leads the editor to reproduce a portion of the Act of Parliament under which the Court was convened. It directs that the Court shall consist of seven members, to be appointed by the King's Commission or under the Great Seal of England, or the seal of the Admiralty of England, directed to all or any of the Admirals, Vice-Admirals, Rear-Admirals, Judges of Vice Admiralty, or Commanders of any of His Majesty's ships of war, and also to all or any such person or persons, officer or officers by name, or for the time being, as His Majesty should think fit to appoint. Which said Commission shall have full power to commit, and to call and assemble a Court of Admiralty, which Court shall consist of seven persons. If so many of the persons aforesaid cannot conveniently be assembled, that any three of the aforesaid persons (whereof the President or Chief of Some English Factory, or the Governor or Lieutenant Governor, or Member of His Majesty's Councils in any of the Plantations or Colonies aforesaid, or Commander of one of His Majesty's ships is always to be one) shall have full power and authority to call and assemble any other persons to make up the number, provided only known Merchants, Factors, Planters, etc., etc., be taken. (Statutes-at-Large, 11, 12; William 3, c. 7, p. 9, 14, 15).

1. This reference is quite incomprehensible.

2. Sylvanus Keach was a brother of Stephen Keach, with whom the exiles were quartered.

six. Clear, cool morning, little wind, northerly.
The Count treated me with chocolate for breakfast.
This morning we spent in shaving and cleaning ourselves, and went through the service of the day.[1]
Some of the family went to meeting. Our dinner
was some of the gammon left yesterday, fried, with
cucumbers, and a cold turn-over pie made with dried
apples and martil berries,[2] a very great curiosity.
I had a nap after dinner, and a bad headack
[ache]. The weather being warm. Our family
seems to be a little more good natured. The coolness seems to wear off gradually, though it's my
opinion there never can be a perfect harmony again.
We drank coffee with the family, and afterwards R.
Beale and I took a walk in the woods and upon the
Hill; returned, ate our bread and milk, chatted till
a quarter before ten, and went to bed.

Monday, August 5, 1776. Arose at twenty minutes after five. A fine, clear morning, little air of

1. Mr. Vernon was the senior warden of Trinity Church, Newport, and
doubtless read the Episcopal service for the day.

2. This word in the manuscript is clearly written as here printed. It is
probably a corruption of whortleberry; subsequently Mr. Vernon writes
W. Berries in some places.

wind, southerly. The mornings and evenings are
grown much cooler than they were. The wind breezed
up before breakfast. For breakfast we had chocolate. We tarried in the house all the forenoon. Our
landlady gave us leave to gather some beans, which
we had for dinner, with salt pork. We prepared
them for the pot, which we always have done. The
weather is warm, and a small nap in the chair was
agreeable. We tarried in the house till between
five and six o'clock, and very dull it is to me, not
having heard from home this ten days. Besides we
have neither books nor company to divert our minds,
which renders this life the more disagreeable. Mr.
Beale, Mr. Lechmere and I took a walk to the river
and gave Mrs. Keach what foul linen we had to
wash. Returned in the evening. Eat baked apples
and milk for supper, and went to bed at a quarter
after nine. N. B.—We killed a snake in the woods
on our way home.

Tuesday, August 6, 1776. The bed being no
longer agreeable, I turned out at five minutes before five. The wind is fair, southerly, and the morning pleasant and clear, but it soon became very

warm and continued so all day. About ten o'clock
Mr. Thomas Lechmere[1] paid us a visit from Newport, and brought Mr. Lechmere some necessaries
and informed us that our families were well. He also
informed us that he was searched about eight o'clock
at the Widow Waterman's[2] by some person unknown
to him, who called himself a Deputy, who opened
and read some letters from our wives, and took one
letter from him directed to his father. He dined
with us upon salt pork, fried, it being the remainder
we had yesterday for dinner, with sliced cucumbers.
He tarried with us till between three and four
o'clock, and returned to Providence with a letter
from us to Governor Cooke complaining of our great
unhappiness, and the uneasiness of the people of the

1. At the trial of the pirates in 1723, Thomas Lechmere, Esq., was in some
way connected with the Court. His official title as then given is Surveyor
General of North America. He was doubtless from Boston. He was probably
the father of Nicholas, Anthony, Thomas (here noted) and Richard, all at the
Revolutionary period resident of Newport, or in some way connected with that
town. All royalists, and all left the Colony, and two at least went to Bristol,
England, from whence they probably came. None of them ever appear to
have been admitted freemen of Rhode Island.

2. This must have been a tavern keeper on the road to Providence from
Newport, and probably not far from the latter. Nevertheless the name of the
Widow Waterman is not to be found in the Road Lists which are attached
to the Almanacs of the period.

town, and desired that he would send us a Pass for
our safe travelling, that we might deliver ourselves
up to the officer for our commitment either to Newport or Providence Gaol, rather than be in this very
disagreeable situation. A dish of tea this afternoon
afforded us a good deal of refreshment. Mr. Nicoll
complains greatly of being very much indisposed.
Took a walk (all of us) to Prospect Hill and returned in the evening. The weather became cloudy,
it looks like rain. Much lightning in the northwest.
We ate our bread and milk, and turned in before ten
o'clock.

Wednesday, August 7, 1776. Arose ten minutes
after five. The wind southwest; cloudy, hazy morning. Mr. Nicoll got up soon after me, and complains
still of being very unwell; is gone out in pursuit of
something to take for his disorder in the bowels.
The sun appeared before seven o'clock, and the wind
breezed up. Our breakfast, coffee. We gathered
some beans and prepared them. Thomas Lechmere
returned from Providence at a quarter before eleven
o'clock, but brought us no written answer from the
Governor, but only a verbal one, that something

would be done for us at the setting of the Assembly. We had a small toddy before dinner. Our dinner consisted of one of our tongues boiled, and a small piece of pork, with carrots from Newport, and the aforesaid beans. T. Lechmere informed us that the persons that robbed and searched him were Corporals Chad Brown[1] and Resolved Waterman[1]; they called themselves Deputies, but showed no authority for their doings. He returned to Newport at three o'clock. We wrote a billet by him to Henry Ward, Esq., requesting of him that he would wait on the Governor for an answer to our letter.[2] It being very warm we tarried in the house till after tea, when Mr. Beale, Mr. Lechmere and myself took a walk southward. The evening was warm and pleasant, but there was lightning in the westward. We ate our milk and bread, and went to bed at half after nine.

Thursday, August 8, 1776. Arose at twenty minutes after five. A cloudy morning; a fresh breeze at S. W.; an appearance of rain. The last night was

1. Chad Brown was a Deputy from Glocester, see note p. 59. Resolved Waterman was not a Deputy.

2. Diligent search of the State archives fails to reveal this letter.

warmer than it has been in the night for some time
past. Our breakfast was tea. The radishes begin to
grow very hard and sticky. It began to rain between
eight and nine o'clock, and continued raining till
four P. M., with some thunder. One Elder Williams[1] and Doctor Hearnton[2] [Harrington] put into ·
our house for shelter. The former of whom was
sulky and did not choose to speak to us, but the
Doctor came into our room, and was very civil and
sociable. Our dinner was a piece of salt pork and a
small piece of salt beef, but the latter not eatable; we
also had some beans, squashes, and a pudding. Half
a tongue left yesterday did not appear at table,
which is a disappointment, especially to Mr. Nicoll,
who did not taste of it yesterday. It ceased raining about four o'clock, and the sun appeared but

1. Elder John Williams was connected with the Baptist (Six Principle)
Church in Foster, near Hopkins' Mills.

2. This name as now spelled is Harrington. In the Rhode Island Records
and other early writings it is spelled in many ways, thus: Herrington, Herren-
deen, Herrinden, Herndeen, Hernden, Herington, Herrenden, Herenden. The
families were very numerous in the northerly towns; at this time there were
eleven families in Glocester, fifteen families in Smithfield, fourteen families in
Scituate, and scattering families in the adjoining towns. There was a physician
by the name living in Smithfield at this period. He practiced there subsequent
to the Revolution.

soon shut in again. The wind at S. E. Mr. Nicoll
being upon the hill to the southward, heard the reports of five or six cannon very distinctly, and half
an hour afterwards as many more. Mr. Lechmere
(also) heard the last reports. The family drank tea
with us; between five and six o'clock it began to
rain again very hard, and continued till eight o'clock.
Our supper, milk and bread; chatted till half after
nine and went to bed.

Friday, August 9, 1776. Arose at half after five;
a very thick, foggy morning, with very little wind;
our breakfast, tea. It began to rain between nine
and ten, and continued till almost twelve, when the
sun appeared. Our dinner was what they call fry'd
lamb, and a very small piece of pork, with some
beans and cucumbers. The weather is very warm
after the rain (which invited a nap in the chair),
and continued so until after five o'clock, when appeared a very sudden gust of wind, with rain, which
continued until sun setting, this cooled the air very
much. Mr. Nicoll, Mr. Beale and myself took a
walk in the evening, when we returned Mr. Lechmere was not at home. He went out soon after we

did, and did not get home till some time after we were gone to bed (being a quarter after nine) which gave us some uneasiness.

Saturday, August 10, 1776. Arose seven minutes before six. Little wind, but very foggy, disagreeable morning. My company not rising very early, I generally spend my time until nigh breakfast with a book, especially when the weather is not agreeable. Our breakfast was tea. The remainder of the forenoon has been employed in the house (by all) except Mr. Nicoll, who always, if he possibly can, takes a walk both before and after dinner. He generally chooses to be alone. About twelve o'clock the sun began to appear, though faintly, and by one o'clock it shined brightly. Very little air of wind, which caused it to be very warm ; our dinner was a forequarter of lamb roasted, with a cheek of pork boiled, with squashes and cucumbers. We dined in the kitchen with the family for the first time. I must observe that our landlord informed us (as he has frequently something that is disagreeable with which to alarm us) that his wife was this day at Neighbor Johnson's wife's groaning,[1] and that the old Granne acquainted the company that the inhabitants of the town were extremely angry with Mr. Keach and his family for entertaining those Tories from Newport, and that they were determined to destroy his house and estate if he persisted in keeping them. At this information Mrs. Keach was much afraid, it gave her much uneasiness. Mr. Nicoll visited Esquire Brown[2] this afternoon, and got the loan of a volume called the Brittanic Constitution, by Roger Acherley.[3] It afforded us much amusement. We drank tea, and afterwards a walk to the river for our linen. Returned in the evening, which was pleasant. Eat our

1. What kind of an entertainment this was the editor has been unable to learn. The term "groaning" was sometimes given to a child-birth, but the "Old Granne" and Neighbor Johnson's recollection of the capture of the Pirates half a century before throws some doubt on that construction.

2. Colonel Chad Brown derives his military title from his connection with the militia. He was a member of the Assembly from Glocester in May, 1776. But he appears to have held the office for six months only. Mr. Brown was a near neighbor, his house being within a quarter of an hour's walk. See Diary, August 20.

3. Roger Acherley, an English lawyer, living in the early part of the eighteenth century, was the author of the work here mentioned on the British Constitution, London, 1727, and of another on Free Parliaments, London, 1731. He published a supplement to his work on the Brittanic Constitution, London, 1780, under the title, Reasons for Uniformity in a State.

milk and bread, chatted till almost ten and went to bed.

Sunday, August 11, 1776. Arose at half after five; a very cloudy, misty morning it is. Breakfast was coffee. Our landlord this morning early sent his youngest son (as he always does on Sundays), about a mile for the Providence newspaper,[1] and the whole forenoon is generally spent in perusing it, and this afternoon in hearing Mr. Johnson read it—such is the fondness of the people for news. This forenoon has been taken up partly in shaving and cleaning ourselves, and each of us a book. Our dinner consisted of a boiled leg of lamb, with pork, squashes and cucumbers; a nap in the chair was not disagreeable this dull, cloudy day. No one of our family (excepting Nicholas, a hired servant,) attended meeting, notwithstanding their great pretention to religion. We tarried in the house all the afternoon, till almost sun setting, when we all took a walk of a circle of three or four miles, notwithstanding the unpleasantness of the weather. Wind about S. E.

---

1. This newspaper was the Providence Gazette, the only newspaper then published in Providence. Saturday was its day of issue. The Newport Mercury was the only other newspaper then published in Rhode Island.

Pudding and milk was given us for supper; went to bed at a quarter after nine.

Monday, August 12, 1776. This morning is wet and cloudy. I did not rise till twenty minutes after six. The wind southerly. Our breakfast, tea. We have been in the house this forenoon; gathered some beans, and prepared them for the pot. Our dinner was a gammon, sent to Mr. Beale from Newport, which our landlady boiled without his or our knowledge, which we could not help remarking as something very extraordinary, as the property was not in her. The forepart of the day was cloudy, flattering weather; in the afternoon showers of rain, at six o'clock a smart one. Cadowza[1] has made two trips this day to read the news, as he usually does. Tea in the afternoon, after which, about half after six, we had the pleasure of seeing Mr. T. Wyatt,[2] from Newport, who brought us some necessaries, and informed us that our families were well. It rained all the

1. This is probably a nickname applied to Neighbor Johnson, so frequently mentioned. Whether the word is a variation of the slang word "catouse," or how it arose, the editor has been unable to discover.

2. Believed to be James Wyatt; see note on page 39.

C

evening. We chatted till ten o'clock and went to bed.

Tuesday, August 13, 1776. Arose at half after six. A cloudy morning, with little wind; the sun soon expelled the thick air, and it became very warm. We breakfasted, all of us, on chocolate; afterwards took a walk with Mr. Wyatt in the woods; picked whortleberries. Our rum being all expended, this two days past, borrowed a gill of our landlady to make some punch Mr. Wyatt having brought a few limes from Providence, a drink of punch (not having tasted any for some time) was a very great comfort to us. Our dinner was a cold rump of beef roasted, a boiled pickled tongue, and the remainder of the cold gammon, with cabbage, the whole of which was sent to us by our friends at Newport, and to crown all, they sent a bottle of Madeira to make our hearts glad. Mr. Wyatt having come in a sulky, and the weather being warm, he was obliged to travel slowly; for these reasons he thought proper to take his leave of us at a quarter after three o'clock; we walked some distance with him; returned and spent the afternoon in the house till evening, when Mr. Beale and I took a walk to the southward, and Mr. Nicoll and Mr. Lechmere went to the river to bathe. Our supper was milk and bread, turned in at a quarter after nine.

Wednesday, August 14, 1776. Arose at a quarter after five. A very thick, foggy morning it is, and calm. It cleared away a good deal before breakfast. Our breakfast was chocolate. We diverted ourselves in the house in the best manner we could all the forenoon. Our dinner was a line of lamb fried, and a piece of salt beef, with squashes, being the bounty of our friends at Newport, with some cherry punch before dinner; a nap was not amiss that cloudy afternoon, which we spent in the house till a quarter after six, when the sun appeared, and we had an agreeable walk. The wind S. E. The evening was starlight. Our supper was milk and bread; went to bed at a quarter before ten.

Thursday, August 15, 1776. Arose at twenty minutes before six. A very wet morning it is, and continued so all the forepart of the day, which gave us an opportunity to settle our accounts with the landlord,[1] who took occasion to inform us that being at Cepagget [Chepachet] on Monday last, in company with one Jonathan Mitchell,[2] who told him that he had thirty or forty men at his command who would enlist and were ready, willing and determined, as soon as he had finished mowing, to come to his house and carry off those Newport people. Our dinner was some of the cold remnants of meat, a piece of pork boiled, with some cabbage and some cucumbers, and a pudding. The afternoon was very thick, cloudy and wet, which caused us to keep in the house. Our supper was pudding and milk. Turned in at twenty minutes after nine.

Friday, August 16, 1776. Arose at twenty minutes after five. The morning is very thick and cloudy, notwithstanding which I walked out about half a mile. Our breakfast was tea. Mr. Beale and I gathered some beans and prepared them for

1. Mr. Keach sent a bill for board of these gentlemen to the Assembly, and was allowed by that body £10 16s. The settlement here mentioned must have been for some extra matters. Mr. Keach's account was for eleven weeks' board of the four persons, or nine shillings each per week.

2. There was a person by this name at this time resident of Gloucester, but his name is not to be found connected in any way with the civil or military government of the State; he must have been a man of no prominence.

the pot. We had them for dinner, with some squashes, and a piece of smoked beef sent by our friends at Newport. It was very good. I can't help remarking that our landlady cooked this beef without our knowledge, a repetition of this kind we think somewhat singular, especially as they took the liberty of cutting off, and retaining the better part before sending it to us. I took a book in my hand after dinner, which induced me to take a short nap in the chair. The wind for the most part of the day has been southerly, but very flattering, uncertain weather. We all took a walk at five o'clock, and in our way we called in at one Mr. Eddy's.[1] This is the first house I have been in (saving our washerwoman's) since we came to this place. The man of the house was not at home, his wife treated us civilly; she is a weaver, and we talked with her about weaving us some handkerchiefs; she expressed a desire to oblige us, but feared that if the people of the town knew it, the consequences might be injurious to her and her family, whereupon the subject

1. There were at this time fifteen families by this name resident in the town of Glocester.

was dropped and we returned home, eat our pudding and milk, and went to bed at ten minutes after nine.

Saturday, August 17, 1776. I arose about five o'clock. The weather is very cloudy, notwithstanding which I found our landlord preparing to set out for Providence with his daughter Winsor. They took their leave of us at twenty minutes after six. Mr. Beale sent a billet unsealed to Mr. Checkley[1] to desire his interest and that of his friends with the members of the Assembly, to get us removed to some town further south, for the convenience of our families. It is true he took the paper after our reading it to him, but we thought very unwillingly. Our breakfast was chocolate. Mr. Beale and I gathered some beans and prepared them for the pot. We had them for dinner, with the remains of a piece of our

1. Mr. William Checkley was a resident of Providence. The Assembly was to be in session at Newport on the following Monday, possibly Mr. Checkley had business there. In 1772 Lieutenant Dudingston, commander of the Gaspee, was lying at Pawtuxet, wounded by a musket ball in the abdomen, received by him during the attack on his vessel. While in this condition he was arrested by the sheriff on a writ, at the suit of Jacob Greene & Co., of East Greenwich. Mr. Checkley hearing of this and knowing the condition of the wounded officer, hurried to Pawtuxet and humanely offered bail to the officers, which was declined; he then apprized the Commissioners of Customs of the fact. (R. I. Col. Rec., vol. vii, p. 87).

smoked beef, and a small pudding. We kept the house all the afternoon till after four o'clock, when we all took a walk to the river for our clean linen. The washerwoman roasted us some ears of corn, for which we paid her. When we got home, it being after sunset we found our landlord and his daughter returned from Providence. He brought us half a gallon of rum, which we paid him for. He told us that he saw the Governor [Cooke], Mr. Henry Ward, and some other gentlemen, but they gave him but little encouragement for our removal. We eat our pudding and milk for supper, and went to bed at a quarter after nine.

Sunday, August 18, 1776. Arose at half after five o'clock. It continues very cloudy weather, with showers in the forepart of the day. The wind about N. E. Our breakfast, tea. After breakfast we shirted and shaved ourselves. Three-quarters after ten o'clock our landlord mounted his horse to wait on Judge Steere,[1] who, he tells us, is going to Newport to-

1. Richard Steere was elected a member of the Assembly from Glocester in August, 1776. He served on some of the committees in 1777, and was, during that year, made one of the Justices of the Court of Common Pleas for Providence County. He held this position until 1781, when he was elected Chief Justice of the same Court, which position he occupied until 1785.

morrow to attend the Assembly. Our landlord will give his account[1] for our board to Judge Steere, to be by him laid before the House. Our landlord further informed us that he should request of Judge Steere to move that we be ordered to some other place. That it was not convenient for him to keep us any longer. Our dinner was one of our landlady's gammons, with squashes. No person from this house attended meeting but poor, honest Christopher.[2] The afternoon was wet and drizzly till four o'clock, when the sun appeared, though faintly; we were glad to see it. I must observe (saving this day) that the whole family have almost lived upon our provisions for eight or nine days past. It seems they can digest Tories' victuals very well, though they pretend that they can't their company nor conversation. Miss Polly Fenner drank tea with us; she was very sociable, and we in return treated her as politely as was in our power. Three of us took a walk, leaving the Count at home; when we returned we found three or four other young women had taken possession of our room. I must observe that in our walk we saw a blacksmith and

1. Already referred to in note on page 64.   2. One of Mr. Keach's hired men.

his assistants hard at work in their shop, which they tell us is very common. Indeed the people will, in their houses, do any kind of work, and even without of doors, if necessary. We had the pleasure of seeing the moon this evening, it being the first time since the change; we ate our milk and bread, chatted till almost ten, and turned in.

Monday, August 19, 1776. Arose exactly at six, and found it a very cloudy, rainy morning, with but little wind at N. E. Our breakfast was tea. Spent the forepart of the day in assisting the Count in fitting his tobacco for snuff, and in other matters of my own for my amusement. Our dinner was the cold gammon remains of yesterday, with some stringed beans, and some boiled (green) corn. The sun appeared, though faintly, at twelve o'clock; the afternoon was pleasant and the evening bright. About three o'clock a woman from Windham in Connecticut (being a stranger) called in. She had thread, etc., to sell. The Count traded with her; she afforded us a good deal of diversion; she tarried about an hour, and went away well pleased with her traffic. We all took a walk in the cool of the even-

ing ; returned, ate our pudding and milk, and went
to bed at a quarter before ten.

Tuesday, August 20, 1776. Arose at a quarter
after five. The wind is southerly, though light.
It is a very thick, foggy, disagreeable morning. I
amused myself with a book until the gentlemen rise,
which I generally practice. Our breakfast, tea,
after which I employed myself in making snuff till
dinner. Dinner was a hog's cheek smoked, with
beans and squashes. The sun appeared about twelve
o'clock, and the weather continued pleasant until
towards sun setting, when it became cloudy, notwithstanding which we were not deprived of our
walk. Supper, milk and bread ; retired at half after
nine.

Wednesday, August 21, 1776. Arose at five minutes after five. Cloudy morning, small wind, southerly. Breakfast, coffee.. After which we all walked
to the river, and delivered our dirty linen to Mrs.
Keach. On our way home we killed a snake. Mr.
Beale and I gathered beans and prepared them for
the pot. We had them for dinner, and with them
some roasted corn, and the remainder of the cheek,

and also a small piece of pork boiled ; this was un-
touched by us. After dinner I had a short nap in
the chair, and amused myself with a book until five.
This day has been very flattering, uncertain weather,
although the sun appeared at twelve, which has been
the case many cloudy days since our stay here. A
fresh wind in the afternoon, southeasterly. We had
a walk in the evening S. and N. Our supper, pudding and milk. Turned in soon after nine.

Thursday, August 22, 1776. Turned out at half
after five. A fine, clear morning ; wind W. N. W. ;
it breezed up before breakfast. Breakfast was chocolate. We shirted and shaved, and delivered each
of us a shirt to the house to be washed. Prepared
some beans which we had for dinner with corn ; we
also had one of our tongues and a piece of pork,
together with some cabbage and some carrots from
Newport. Mrs. Keach and the two girls dined with
us in our room. Had a small nap in the chair while
the Count was making snuff. We diverted ourselves
in the house in the best manner we could till tea
time, and afterwards walked to the river to get our
linen. This has been the pleasantest day we have

had for three weeks past. Our supper, pudding and milk. Chatted till about half after nine, and went to bed.

Friday, August 23, 1776. I got up twenty minutes before six. The wind, though small, is about N. W. A cool morning. I amused myself with a book until my company appeared. Our breakfast was chocolate. Afterwards assisted the Count in making his snuff and preparing some beans, which we had for dinner, together with some squashes and also a small piece of pork and a small piece of beef. I assisted the Count in making snuff until tea. Mr. Nicoll walked out this morning, and visited Esquire Williams who was not at home, but the family received him kindly. This afternoon he strolled again, and diverted us with a story of his narrow escape from being caught in a bird net. The net sprung and two men started out from behind a bush and surprised him much. Some words ensued on the occasion, and he thought proper to leave them. We had a very pleasant walk this evening all together. It being a remarkably fine day and evening, neither too warm, nor much wind. My supper was baked apples and milk ; retired at three-quarters after nine.

Saturday, August 24, 1776. Turned out at five minutes after five. A fine, pleasant morning, but rather a cool air; northerly. I amused myself with a book until our gentlemen got up. Breakfast, chocolate, after which I proposed a walk to Mr. Beale, and we set out at twenty-five minutes after eight. We went as far as Esquire Williams's. His wife told us that he was in the field at work, and would have sent for him but we would not suffer it. She treated us with a bowl of toddy. With much civility we took our leave of Mrs. Williams at a quarter before eleven, and got home at twelve. Our dinner was a tongue from Newport, boiled, and with it a piece of pork with some corn and beans. It's not to be doubted but that we ate very heartily after our walk, and a nap was mighty agreeable. Afterwards took a book in my hand. The afternoon being cloudy we tarried in the house till almost six o'clock, and then took a walk to the northward of two miles. Our supper, milk and bread; chatted till nine and went to bed.

Sunday, August 25, 1776. Arose at twenty-five minutes after five. And a fine, agreeable morning

7

it is ; light wind, northerly. Our landlord is preparing to go to Chestnut Hill. Our breakfast, chocolate. Shaved and cleaned ourselves. Amused
myself with a book a great part of the morning.
Our dinner was some very ordinary salt fish and
some spar (sic) [Spanish] potatoes. Our two girls,
with Stephen, for the first time (since our arrival)
attended meeting.   At half after   three James
Wyatt¹ came to us from Newport. He left our
families well, and brought a copy of the act of Assembly empowering the Deputy Sheriff of this town
to remove us to some other house in the town.² He

1. See note on page 39 as to the identity of James with T. Wyatt.

2. This act is as follows :

"IT IS VOTED AND RESOLVED, That Benjamin Smith, Deputy Sheriff of
the County of Providence, be and he is hereby ordered forthwith to remove
Richard Beale, John Nicoll, Nicholas Lechmere and Thomas Vernon from the
house and farm of Stephen Keach to some other house or houses within the
town of Glocester, agreeable to an act of this Assembly, made and passed
at their session, holden in June, A. D. 1776. That unless the said Richard
Beale, John Nicoll, Nicholas Lechmere and Thomas Vernon pay the expences
of their removal and for their board and maintenance in said town, that their
several and respective real estates be taken into possession by the Sheriff
for the County of Newport in behalf of this State. That the aforesaid Richard
Beale, John Nicoll, Nicholas Lechmere and Thomas Vernon have liberty to
remove their families to be with them in said town, and to hire at their own
expence any house or houses in said town to live or reside in, upon condition
that they give their promise in writing to the Sheriff of said County of Provi-

drank tea with us, and afterwards we took a walk all together. Returned, had some bread and milk, chatted till almost ten, and went to bed.

Monday, August 26, 1776. Arose at twenty minutes after six. Wind at S. E. ; a very thick, cloudy morning. It rained very hard before daylight. The sun appeared before nine o'clock. Our breakfast, chocolate. We diverted ourselves in the house until dinner. Our dinner consisted of a gammon from my house in Newport (which was boiled without our

dence that they will not depart from said town of Glocester without license first had and obtained from this Assembly, which said Sheriff is hereby empowered to take such promise accordingly. And it is further

"VOTED AND RESOLVED, That the said Nicholas Lechmere be and he is hereby permitted to reside in any town in the State of Connecticut that he shall choose, first having liberty from the Committee of such town, and giving his parole to observe the restrictions he shall be laid under by such committee." (Acts and Resolves, R. I. Gen. Assem., August, 1776, p. 160.)

Following this order the Assembly, at its September session, further

"VOTED AND RESOLVED, That Mr. Daniel Owen be and he is hereby appointed to procure suitable and convenient places within the town of Glocester for Richard Beale, Thomas Vernon and John Nicoll, and that he immediately remove them to such places accordingly." (Acts and Resolves, R. I. Gen. Assem., September, 1776, p. 177.)

The Deputy Sheriff in regard to the first order made return to the Governor (see this Diary, September 6,) : "That it was not in his power to provide other quarters for the gentlemen on account of the indisposition of the people to take them." There is no return to the second order.

knowledge) and with it some corn and beans. Mr. Wyatt set out from the house at a quarter past two and we parted with him at Esquire Brown's at half after two. The wind about N. E. It began to rain at five, and continued until we went to bed. Our supper, milk and bread. We turned in soon after nine.

Tuesday, August 27, 1776. Arose exactly at six. A very thick, cloudy, sour morning. Our breakfast, chocolate. This being the day for the choice of Deputies[1] (members of the General Assembly). We are told that there is a very great resort of people of all kinds at Chepasseh,[2] and that it is a day of great frolicking. Our landlord and his three sons

1. Members of the Assembly and the Assistants or Senators were elected twice in each year, in April and in August. General officers were elected annually. This arrangement was continued until the adoption of the Constitution, in 1842.

2. The name of the village of Chepachet appears twice in this Diary. It is spelled differently each time, thus: August 15, *Cepagget*; August 27, *Chepasseh*. Parsons' *Indian names* gives the derivation and meaning of this word Chepuck *Devil* and *Chack Bag*, and relates a legendary account of a bag or wallet's having been found, and as no one could tell how it came there, an Indian said it must have been the Devil who dropped it. Williams, in his Key to the Indian Language, gives no such words. The similarity of the word Chack to the English word Sack seems to lead almost to the conclusion that one was a corruption from the other.

are gone, having rigged themselves out in the best
manner.   I must observe that a man on horseback
passed by (together with many others) with a very
large bag full of cakes made by Granne West
(mother to the General)[1] which are to be sold to

1. GEN. WILLIAM WEST.—The family from which this gentleman descended
seems to have dwelt in the southern portion of the Colony of Rhode Island.
Mr. West removed from North Kingstown previously to 1758, for in that year
he was a licensed tavern keeper in the town of Scituate. In 1761 he was
elected a member of the Assembly from that town, and again in 1771 and 1773.
In 1774 meetings were held throughout the Colony for resisting the imposition
of the Tax on tea by Parliament. Mr. West was the moderator of the meeting
in Scituate, and was elected a member of the Committee on Correspondence.
In 1775, in consequence of a threatened attack by the British on Newport, a
force was sent to repel them. Mr. West was placed second in command of this
force, Esek Hopkins being first. He was commissioned Brigadier General of
Militia by the Committee of Safety during the recess of the General Assembly.
While in command at Middletown a dispute arose between Colonels Babcock
and Richmond relative to rank. This affair General West referred to the
Assembly in a letter. About the same time complaints against West were
made on account of his arrests of persons who in his judgment conducted
themselves inimical to the cause of the Colony. The persons so arrested were
Colonel Joseph Wanton, Joseph Aplin, Benjamin Brenton, Joseph Allen and
Nathaniel Case. The Assembly, after a full hearing, dismissed the prisoners
to return to their homes, but at the same time voted, "That it is nevertheless
the opinion of this Assembly that the said General West hath acted therein as
an officer having the Love of his country at heart; and that this Assembly will
ever approve the conduct of their Military Commanders in exerting themselves
for the securing and bringing to trial all persons conducting in a suspicious
manner, at the same time carefully observing not to encroach upon, infringe or
supersede the civil authority by exertions of the military." This course was

the people. I diverted myself this forenoon in finishing a horn tinder-box. Our dinner consisted of
a small piece of cold gammon, cut from that boiled
yesterday (the residue being eaten by the family)
with some squashes. I dare say this gammon
weighed twelve pounds, and that we ate not more
than two pounds of it. The day being very cold

unsatisfactory to General West, it being considered by him as tending to
impair his authority, whereupon he tendered his resignation as Brigadier
General, which was accepted by the Assembly. He was soon after appointed
one of the State committee to procure arms and equipments. In this same
year, 1776, he served the town of Scituate as a member of the Assembly, and
his name is recorded as one of the signers of the famous Declaration by which
Rhode Island severed her connection with the British Crown. He was soon
after appointed to command the third regiment of militia, a position to which
he was annually appointed for several years. In obedience to a request from
the Continental Congress to number the inhabitants, so that the effective
military strength of the State might be known, General West was one of those
appointed by the Assembly to obtain the facts. Later in the same year he was
appointed, together with General Varnum, to assist Malmedy in a system of
fortification for the State. Congress soon after superseded this commission by
the appointment of Continental officers. The Assembly, after reciting the
facts upon which their action was based, passed the following: " Wherefore
this Assembly, retaining a very grateful sense of General West's zeal in the
cause of his country and of his conduct as an officer; and not doubting his
utmost exertions in their service on any future occasion, hereby resolve that he
be, and hereby is dismissed from the office of Brigadier General in the service
'of the State." He was soon after appointed to distribute the bounties to the
soldiers of Scituate, and for this purpose was supplied with upwards of two
thousand pounds. Later in the year the freemen of Scituate becoming dis-

and drizzly, we tarried in the house till after five. Drank tea, having sent for some of the aforesaid cakes, which were pretty good. Took a small walk to the northward, the wind being about N. Our supper, bread and milk. After eight o'clock our landlord came into our room and informed us that he had seen the Deputies of this town, and that they

satisfied with the unequal representation under the Charter, instructed their delegation in the Assembly to procure an act establishing a form of government in which representation should be upon the basis of population and property. The ground taken was that by the Declaration of Independence the Charter became void; and that the power which had vested in the King, now vested in the people; and that the people had since that event authorized or fixed no form of government. General West was one of the committee which drafted these instructions. After the battle of Rhode Island General West received from the Assembly upwards of three thousand pounds for distribution to his regiment for their services during that campaign. In 1779 General West for the third time received the commission of Brigadier General, this time serving under General Varnum. In 1780 he was returned a member of the Assembly from his town, and soon after elected Deputy Governor, serving in that capacity one year. In 1784 and in 1785 he was again sent by his townsmen to the Assembly, which service seems to have closed his public labors, save only as a member of a convention held at East Greenwich in 1786, for the purpose of regulating the prices of merchandize in the State. Soon after his removal to Scituate, General West purchased the farm whereon Stephen and Esek Hopkins were born. Here he built in 1775 a large and excellent house, and carried on the business of farming upon a large scale. This house is still occupied. The terrible depreciation of the Continental and State currency played sad havoc with the pecuniary fortunes of the patriots of the Revolution, and General West was no exception. He died at his homestead about 1816.

told him that the General Assembly had ordered the
Sheriff to remove us to some other house in Glocester, and that we were to pay the charge of our
board, etc., and that if we paid his demands it would
prevent our estate from being attached for that purpose.   We told him in answer to what he said, that
we thought it very extraordinary and unprecedented
that the Assembly should pass an act to look back.[1]
Besides, that we had not had provisions provided
since we had been at his house which were fitting
and proper for us, and that if we had not received
frequent supplies from Newport we should have well
nigh starved.   He being conscious of the truth of

1. The act passed by the Assembly in August, sixty days after the act banishing these gentlemen, imposed penalties which were not imposed by the first
act. These penalties or obligations were made operative from the date of the
first act, and were thus retroactive.   There was nothing contained within the
Charter prohibiting such laws. When Rhode Island adopted the Constitution
of the United States, she was prohibited by the clause in the Constitution from
the passage of such laws. Whereupon the General Assembly resolved that
" Retrospective laws punishing offences committed before the existence of
such laws are oppressive and unjust and ought not to be made." (This is section eight of the Bill of Rights, Laws of Rhode Island, Digest of 1798, p. 81).
That in expressing an opinion that such an action by the Assembly of Rhode
Island was either extraordinary or unprecedented, Mr. Vernon clearly exhibits
his ignorance concerning this distinguished body. This body not only made
the laws, and established courts to administer justice under the laws; but it

this assertion made us no reply, but went out of the room. We sat up till after nine, and turned in.

Wednesday, August 28, 1776. Arose at a quarter after six. It was a very cold night, and so is the morning. The wind about N. W. The sun appeared, though very dull; the weather not yet clear and settled. Our breakfast was coffee. Afterwards shaved ourselves. I amused myself this day in making a powder horn. Our dinner was a small remnant of our cold gammon and a piece of salt pork boiled, which we could not eat an ounce of. We also had some cabbage, and some Spanish potatoes and an Indian pudding, boiled. About the middle of the afternoon the weather cleared and it

---

executed its own laws; punished the judges who ventured to put a construction upon the laws different from such constructions as it wished; annulled the judgments of courts and expunged their records. It wielded for two centuries unlicensed power. The Code of 1647 provided that no person should be taken or imprisoned, or disseized of his lands or liberties, or be exiled, or any otherwise molested or destroyed but by the lawful judgment of his peers, *or by some known law,* and according to the letter of it, ratified and confirmed by the major part of the General Assembly, lawfully met and orderly managed. *(Proceedings of the First Gen. Assem., 1647, p. 18).* The phraseology of this act was altered in March, 1663, so that it read " but by the lawful judgment of his peers, or *by the law of the Colony,*" and secondly, no man should be disseized of his lands or property, or be imprisoned or otherwise molested but by due course of law.

was somewhat warmer. We all took a walk round Mr. Fenner's land, a circle of three or four miles. After we returned, our landlady sent us in a large earthen pan almost full of milk. We could not help remarking on the extraordinary allowance. We imagine it proceeds in consequence of our conversation with the landlord the last evening. This evening was remarkably clear and bright. We chatted till a few minutes after nine and went to bed.

Thursday, August 29, 1776. Arose twenty-five minutes after six. The wind at the N. E. A very cloudy, cold, sour morning, and drizzly. Our breakfast, chocolate. Mr. Nicol and Mr. Beale took a walk out. Mr. Lechmere and myself diverted ourselves in the house, the weather not being very inviting. Our landlady this morning ordered two fowls to be killed, which were boiled, also a piece of pork, some squash, some carrots and some roast corn, for our dinners. This very extraordinary provision we imagine proceeds from our conversation the evening before the last. This day has been very dark and showery for the most part of the time. We attempted to walk the latter part of the afternoon, but were obliged to put back for the rain. We had a good allowance of pudding and milk for our suppers. But notwithstanding, there seems to be a great coolness and indifference towards us. But from what cause it proceeds we know not. The moon appeared in the evening and also some stars. We chatted till three-quarters after nine, when we went to bed very quietly.

Friday, August 30, 1776. Arose at five minutes before six. A very thick, foggy morning, with but little wind. Our breakfast. tea. After breakfast the fog began to clear away. We heard accidentally that our landlord had sent his son Jeremiah to Benjamin Smith, the Deputy Sheriff, respecting our removal, and we hearing at the same time that Smith had been to Providence, and we being unable to obtain any information from the family, Mr. Beale and I, at half-past nine, set out for Mr. Smith's house. We saw him; he was an entire stranger to us; however he treated us very civilly He informed us that he had not been to Providence but to Petuet.[1] Neither had he received any orders

1. Either Pawtucket or Pawtuxet.

respecting us; when he did receive orders he would acquaint us as soon as possible. In short, he gave us all the satisfaction we could desire from a stranger. On our way home we met with Esquire Brown (Mr. Nicol having joined us) whom we had a good deal of chat with. We esteem this man as our best friend in this town. We reached home at twelve, when the Count made us some grog. The day is warm and pleasant. Our dinner, a piece of pork and a small piece of smoked cheek, boiled, with some corn and beans, and some roasted corn. At three o'clock we went to the Hall, after some time Mr. Nicol joined us, and at five o'clock we took a walk southward, in a circle of three miles. Returned home in the evening, it being cloudy, though very calm all day. Ate our pudding and milk, and went to bed at a quarter before ten.

Saturday, August 31, 1776. Arose at a quarter before six. Clear, pleasant morning; wind northerly. The first object that presented itself to our vision was our landlord; dressed in his Sabbath day clothes, with his horse, on which he presently mounted. He said nothing to us but rode away.

We were told afterwards that he was gone to Providence. I amused myself this forenoon in finishing my powder horn. We had a smart shower just before ten, which continued half an hour; our dinner was some salt fish and some potatoes, both of which were as bad of the kind as you can possibly conceive. I had a small nap after dinner. The weather is clear and fine. All the male kind, excepting ourselves, being away from home, the women, to do them justice, appeared to be good natured and obliging, I suppose with the thought of our parting with them soon. We all took a walk to ye northward; when we returned we ate our milk and bread, and went to bed at a quarter before ten. It is a fine evening.

Sunday, September 1, 1776. Arose at half after six. A very serene, agreeable morning; light wind, northerly. Who should be in our room but the landlord reading the newspaper. He informed me that he had been to Providence, and that he saw Mrs. Vernon at N. Angell's house.[1] She came up

1. Nicholas Angell was a butcher; he lived in Providence, and for many years kept a market.

from Newport the day before with other company. Our landlord brought with him the order[1] respecting our removal, which he sent to Benjamin Smith, the Deputy Sheriff. Our breakfast, tea. Soon after breakfast we all set out to see Mr. Smith, whom we found at home. Our treatment was kind, and he was very much inclined to oblige us. But he thought it would be very difficult to procure lodgings for us, for that all the people he had talked with were not fond of taking us in. He informed us also that he should go to Providence on Wednesday next. We parted with him after eleven o'clock and reached home exactly at twelve. The weather being warm, a drink of grog was not amiss. For our dinner we had one of their gammons. It was very salt and badly cured; we also had some squashes and some boiled corn. Our landlady and her daughter Freelove dined with us. The landlord and his two sons being gone over the river to make their hay. Patty and the youngest son went to meeting. It became cloudy after twelve o'clock, and looked like rain. We had tea in the afternoon, after which we all took

1. This order is given in note on page 74.

a walk to the southward. Returned in the evening, which was pleasant and agreeable. Ate our milk and bread, and went to bed at half after nine.

Monday, September 2, 1776. Got up this morning at a quarter after six. A very fine, clear sky, and a light air. Our breakfast, chocolate. Mr. Nicoll and myself took a long circular walk to the westward of five or six miles. The weather being warm, we were much fatigued. We returned just at twelve, found Mr. Beale and Mr. Lechmere in good spirits. They gave us a drink of grog, which was mighty refreshing. Our dinner was some sliced gammon, fried, the remains from yesterday's dinner, with corn and beans, and some roasted corn. The walk encouraged me to take a nap. The weather became cloudy in the afternoon, and the wind turned from S. W. to N. W., with the weather cooler. The Count proposed a dish of tea, at which there was not one negative voice. We ate our pudding and milk at eight, and went to bed soon after nine.

Tuesday, September 3, 1776. Arose at ten minutes before six. The weather not clear. Our landlord informed us that B. Smith intended to start for

Providence this day. We ate our breakfast, being chocolate, shaved, and Mr. Beale, Mr. Lechmere, and myself took a walk to see him. He told us that he should set out at one o'clock. I gave him a letter to Mrs. Vernon. We reached home at twelve, found it very warm, though not much sun. The wind S. W. Met Mr. Nicol on our way. A little grog was not amiss. Our dinner was a piece of salt pork, which was very fat, a small piece of beef so bad that we could not possibly eat it, with some squashes, so that we were obliged to make our dinner on a small piece of cheese and some bread. The weather being warm, we tarried in the house till after tea, which our landlady ordered unasked, being conscious that we ate very little dinner. We took a walk at five o'clock to the southward and to Prospect Hill, where we had the pleasure of seeing the sun set very clear. We tarried upon the hill till after dark. When we got home we ate our pudding and milk at eight, as usual, and went to bed at a quarter after nine, it being a warm, agreeable night.

Wednesday, September 4, 1776. Arose at eight minutes before six ; a very fine, clear, agreeable morning. The wind northwesterly. Having occasion to go into the kitchen before breakfast (which consisted of chocolate) I perceived that our landlady had ordered two or three chickens to be killed, we suppose to make amends for yesterday's dinner, which I am sure we did not eat an ounce of. I tarried in the house this forenoon. Our dinner, three chickens, baked in the oven, with apple sauce and Spanish potatoes. This was a feast to us, though badly cooked. The women are cheerful and good natured, I suppose with the hope of our leaving them soon. I amused myself in the house till after five o'clock, when we walked to the southward and to Prospect Hill. Our supper, pudding and milk; we turned in at a quarter after nine. A very fresh wind from N. W. since nine o'clock.

Thursday, September 5, 1776. Arose at eight minutes before six. A very cool night and the morning is clear. A breeze from the northwest. Breakfast, tea. Our landlord bought a side of lamb. The family are determined that we shall part good friends, which is our hearty wish, having done everything to promote a good harmony in our power. Mr.

Beale and Mr. Nicol walked to B. Smith's this forenoon, but they found he had not returned from Providence. The Count and I gathered beans for dinner,
which consisted of a part of the forequarter of lamb,
with some pork baked, followed by a rice pudding.
We tarried in the house till five o'clock, when we
took a walk to the southward in expectation of meeting with a Newport friend. The wind came from
the eastward before night, pleasant although cool.
We ate bread, peaches and milk, and turned in at
half after nine.

Friday, September 6, 1776. Arose two minutes
before six. A very pleasant, agreeable morning;
small wind, about N. W. We shaved ourselves
before breakfast (which consisted of tea) and soon
after walked to B. Smith's house, which is about
one and three-quarters of a mile distant. He was
not returned from Providence. We chatted with his
wife above an hour; she was very sociable. We
reached home at eleven o'clock. The weather is
warm, which gave us a relish for a drink of grog.
Our dinner was a boiled leg of lamb and pork, with
squashes and carrots. Had a nap in the chair. About

three o'clock Mrs. Vernon and William Bardin made
their appearance. You may rest assured they were
very welcome visitors. We got them dinner, and
made some punch with limes which they brought
with them. They also brought us some refresh-
ments. We had a dish of tea, and you may suppose
a good deal of chat with respect to our friends at
Newport. We walked to the northward in the evening, and met Mr. B. Smith. He told us that our
Petition[1] was rejected by the Lower House of Assembly by three or four votes. That he-had delivered the last order of Assembly to the Governor
(Cooke) in person, with a return thereon, that it
was not in his power to procure any quarters for us
in the town of Glocester on account of the disposition of the people, and that had no further concern
with us, having received no fresh instructions.
Neither could the Governor direct him what was
to be done with us. Upon which he took his leave
of His Honor and came home.[2] He walked with us

1. Careful search among the archives of the State, as preserved in the office
of the Secretary of State, disclose neither this petition, nor any of the letters
which the Diary informs us were written to the Governor. Nor can any of the
orders of the Committee of Safety with reference to these men now be found.

2. Referred to in note on page 75.

to our lodgings, and parted with us after eight
o'clock with a good disposition to oblige us. Our
supper was milk, bread and peaches. Went to bed
before ten.

Saturday, September 7, 1776. Arose at five minutes after six. A cloudy morning, and drizzles.
The wind about S., but small. Our landlord set
out for Providence this morning early, to wait on
the Assembly respecting his pay for our board.[1]
Our breakfast, tea. Soon after breakfast packed up
our clothes and prepared to set out for Providence,
but waited for Mr. Bardin's return from Esquire
Williams's. It was thirty-five minutes after nine before we took our leave of the family. We walked
about five miles when our company had a parley,
and came to a resolution of a separation. Mr. Lechmere,[2] Mr. Bardin and Mrs. Vernon proceeded to
Providence, and Messrs. Nicol, Beale and Vernon
took the Scituate road with a determination to proceed to Newport. We travelled seven miles further
without any refreshment to the house of one Joseph
Fisk, upon the borders of Cranston. Two small

1. Referred to in note on page 64.　　2. Here we take leave of Mr. Lechmere.

showers happened in the mean time. This house could only give us some cider, brandy, grog—bad of the kind. We tarried about half an hour, and at nearly one o'clock proceeded on our journey. The weather being very drizzly and wet. At Shanticut,[1] being obliged to stop under a large net to shelter us from the rain, we were joined by four Scotch officers who had been sent from Newport into exile about the time we were.[2] We conversed with them until the rain ceased. We then took our leave of them, and arrived at the Fulling Mill[3] about half after five, being very wet and uncomfortable. Some cherry rum and grog was mighty agreeable. A bit of cold tongue which Mr. Beale had in his pocket was all the food we had eaten since breakfast. The weather still continued very wet, notwithstanding which we persevered in our walk. Before we arrived at East Greenwich it became very dark;

1. Shanticut is probably an abbreviation of the word Moshanticut, which was the Indian name of a brook. This brook empties into the Pawtuxet river above the Pocasset brook. The hamlet now known as the Ore Bed is doubtless the situation referred to.

2. There is no mention in the Acts and Resolves of these Scotch officers. They may have been exiled by the Committee of Safety, or by the Council of War during a recess of the Assembly.

3. The Fulling Mill is the present village of Apponaug.

however we procured a man to put us over the cove
to Richard Greene's[1] land, where we had about a
mile to walk to his house. We arrived before nine
o'clock. Our friend was gone to bed, but he soon
made his appearance. He gave us a hearty and kind
welcome; provided us with dry clothing and every
other refreshment we could wish or desire. We
chatted till about eleven o'clock, when we went to
bed. I was very restless and uneasy in the night
which proceeded, I imagine, from my supper, although it consisted only of a bit of chicken.

Sunday, September 8, 1776. Arose at half after
seven, having overslept from fatigue of the walk.

1. Richard Greene was born October 4, 1725; he died July 17, 1779; he
married Sarah, daughter of Thomas and Mercy [Greene] Fry; she died April
4, 1775. For genealogy of this family, see the close of this Tract. Mr. Greene
was afflicted with a cancer, from which he died; he received permission from the
Assembly to visit Newport, while that town was in possession of the British,
to obtain the services of an English surgeon. The remedies were unsuccessful.
Mr. Greene was a Royalist, and at the breaking out of the Revolution espoused
the cause of the English, and although he owned large amounts of produce, he
declined to dispose of it for the use of the rebels; in consequence of this
refusal the Assembly appointed James Arnold, Jr., to purchase Mr. Greene's
corn, oats, rye, pork and sheep for the use of the State. If Mr. Greene refused
to sell, Mr. Arnold was directed to seize the produce, pay for it the prices
which the Assembly had fixed, and remove it to a place of safety. Mr. Greene,
like many of the large farmers in the Narragansett country, lived in truly
baronial style. His estate is now known as Potowomut.

Though much better than I could expect to find myself from the badness of the weather, the badness of the road, and the distance of the walk. The weather this forenoon has been rainy, cloudy, and very uncertain. Mr. Greene has been kind enough to send out in search of a boat for us to proceed to Newport, but can hear of none that will sail before morning. We spent this day very agreeably, having an excellent dinner provided for us and a kindly welcome. Being in bed about one hour and a half. Between eleven and twelve (the night of Sunday) we were surprised in our sleep by a knocking at the door. Mr. Greene got up, opened his window, and was soon made acquainted with the fact that a party had come in pursuit of us. The party numbered about twelve persons, some of whom were armed. One of whom, Richard Greene, introduced to our bedroom. His name was Jacob Greene[1]; soon

1. Jacob Greene was the elder brother of General Nathanael Greene. He was a member of the firm of Greene & Co., of East Greenwich. This firm was engaged in commercial pursuits. It was one of their vessels which Lieutenant Dudingston in the Gaspee had seized in 1772, and for which act the firm brought a suit in trover, and arrested Lieutenant Dudingston as he lay wounded at Pawtuxet. This arrest took place two days after he was shot, June 12, 1772. The case was tried in the Court of Common Pleas in the fol-

afterwards Stephen Mumford[1] (of the party) came in. They told us that they were informed that we had broke the laws of the General Assembly by departing from the town of Glocester without leave of the authorities. We told them exactly our case, and our reasons for leaving the town we were detained in, and that we much preferred a gaol to the hard treatment we had received, and for that purpose took the resolution to proceed to Newport and there to deliver ourselves into the possession of the Sheriff of that county for commitment. Much alter-

---

lowing month. Judgment was given against Dudingston. The case was appealed to the Superior Court. It came on for trial in October, when, on account of a violent storm, the counsel for Dudingston not being able to cross the ferries it went by default. His counsel petitioned the Assembly for a new trial. The petition was granted; a new trial resulted in another judgment against Dudingston. A few days later the amount of the execution was paid, and the receipt signed by Nathanael Greene & Co., per Christopher Greene, notwithstanding which Arnold says General Nathanael Greene was not a party in the case. The vessel which Dudingston seized, belonging to Greene & Co., was condemned in Boston. Judgment went against Dudingston in Rhode Island because he sent the vessel beyond the jurisdiction of Rhode Island for trial. The vessel was condemned because she was engaged in illegal traffic. When General Greene became Quartermaster-General, he appointed his brother Jacob Commissary of purchases for Rhode Island. Mr. Greene died suddenly of apoplexy while on business at Bristol, November 8, 1811, in his sixty-ninth year.

1. Stephen Mumford was a prominent man living at East Greenwich. He was a member of the Committee of Safety for 1776.

cation ensued, and finally it was determined that we should appear in the town of East Greenwich in the morning, after breakfast, to confer further on the subject. With this arrangement we pledged our words of honor that we would comply, and they took their leave of us.

Monday, September 9, 1776. We arose before six. Ate our breakfast, and prepared ourselves to meet the gentlemen who had waited upon us during the night previous. After eight o'clock Mr. Greene accompanied us down to the cove and then returned home. We passed over the said cove in a canoe, paddled by a boy. We went to the house of Mr. Arnold, a tavern, where we waited some time for the gentlemen. At last they appeared, viz., Major Mumford, Jacob Greene, Major P'd Peirce,[1] and one Runnolds. We interceded with them greatly, as we had done the night before, for our liberty to proceed to Newport; we offered to give any security

1. Major Preserved Peirce or Pearce was an officer in the militia; his daughter Mary married, November 2, 1775, Major John Singer Dexter, who served in the Continental army, in the Rhode Island regiment under Colonel Christopher Greene, and afterwards under Colonel Jeremiah Olney. Major Peirce served his town as a Deputy at several periods.

9

they desired that we would there deliver ourselves into the custody of the Sheriff, he to do with us what he thought best. But all the arguments we could make use of was to no purpose. Finally they concluded to send an express to Providence, with a letter to Governor Cooke, asking his orders respecting us, since we would not agree upon an explanation of the Act of Assembly. Accordingly Major Peirce set off about twelve o'clock. They were so obliging as to consent that we should write a letter to the Governor, which we did. (But these gentlemen were not so kind as to let us know by what authority they exercised this power over us.) We requested of the Governor that he would give orders for our release, and that we be sent to Newport, subject to such restrictions as the law directs. We spent the day at Arnold's tavern, and retired to bed at half after nine.

Tuesday, September 10, 1776. Arose about six o'clock. After breakfast Major Preserved Peirce waited on us to let us know that he delivered our letter to the Governor, but received no answer in writing, the Governor giving for a reason that he was just going to the Small Pox Hospital,[1] and had not time to write. But the Governor told him that we must be ordered to Providence (by whom) Gaol forthwith agreeably to an act of Assembly.[2] An act of which we never before had knowledge. Accordingly we set off for Providence at a quarter after ten o'clock, on foot, having been denied the liberty of going by water, notwithstanding an opportunity presented itself. Elder Gorton[3] was just about leaving for Providence with his boat and would gladly have received us on board, but all the arguments and en-

1. Small Pox Hospitals were at this time (1776) being erected under a State law. Persons were inoculated with small pox, the law declaring that the distemper taken by inoculation is so easy and light and the method of treatment so beneficial, that persons so inoculated are more likely to live than those not inoculated, and that by the introduction of the practice the greater portion of the male inhabitants will soon get over the disease.

2. Nothing contained in the act directed the taking of these men to Providence. It simply directs that if they broke their parole they were to be committed to gaol—but to no particular county. The transaction was entirely without even the formality of law.

3. Elder John Gorton, an earnest preacher of the Six Principle Baptist sect, was ordained pastor of the East Greenwich Church, September 6, 1753. He remained in this connection until his death, June 6, 1792. He was the servant not only of his congregation but of the whole town. During a large portion of the time he was the only ordained minister in the neighborhood, and therefore he joined in marriage many of the neighboring people. His Record of Marriages, nearly three hundred, has recently been printed.

treaties we could make use of were of no effect.
The weather was very warm, and we were unpre-
pared for such a tedious walk; however, we persevered; we stopped but once on our way, and that
was at the house of one John Rice Arnold. This
house was about half the distance of our walk. It
was a private house. Mr. Arnold made us a drink
of grog. He provided us with some fried bacon or
pork and eggs, with some bread and cheese. For
this he would receive no pay though strongly urged.
We left this family and house after resting ourselves
some time, and arrived at Providence about four
o'clock in the afternoon; we were then committed
to gaol, and entered on the books by Paul Tew,[1] Esquire, the High Sheriff of the county. In the presence
of one Jonathan Niles, Deputy Sheriff of the County of Kent, and who lives in West Greenwich, and
John Stafford, of Warwick, his assistant. The two

1. The earliest mention of this person appears to be his appointment by
Governor Stephen Hopkins to transport prisoners to Nova Scotia in 1758. In
these commissions one man to each ton was allowed on the vessels. Mr. Tew
was Sheriff of Providence County almost continuously from 1761 to 1778. In
this capacity immense amounts of property captured by privateers sailing from
Narragansett Bay in 1776 and 1777, and owned by Rhode Island people, passed
through his hands.

persons who escorted us to this dismal, disagreeable place.[1] It is full of people, being much overcrowded. It has not the conveniences of bed or bedding. Seven of us were lodged in one small room. There were many other shocking circumstances too tedious to mention. We questioned our guards above mentioned with respect to their power of taking us into custody, and committing us. They acknowledged that they had no legal process from any magistrate to take us into custody, nor for our commitment, saving a copy of the act of Assembly, passed at the session in July, 1776.[2] We made ourselves as easy as possible in this shocking situa-

1. This jail was the fourth one built in Providence. It was built in 1753, and it ceased to be used as a prison in 1799. It stood near where the Central Police Station now stands. However willing these men were to be committed while they were in Glocester, it is noticeable that once having a taste of life there, they used every immediate effort to get back into the country, and then took special pains not to break their parole again. These jails were a disgrace to humanity.

2. There was no act concerning these men in any way passed by the Assembly at its July session, 1776. The only act indirectly concerning them was an act providing that no male person should have the right to petition the Assembly to set aside the judgment of a court, or stay an execution. Neither should he possess the right to bring a suit or action before any Court of Record within the State, unless he had previously signed or subscribed to the Declaration or Test Act. This Test Act may be found in the Introduction to this Tract. (*Acts and Resolves, R. I. Gen. Assem., July, 1776, p. 158*).

tion, but the night was very tedious, with but little rest or sleep.

Wednesday, September 11, 1776. I arose at six o'clock, after a very uncomfortable night. We breakfasted with the company belonging to the house, on chocolate. Henry Ward, Esquire, (the Secretary of State) came to see us, which we took very kind. He informed us of the committee[1] sitting at Newport the morrow on public business during the recess of the General Assembly, and advised us by all means to prefer our petition to that committee for our relief or removal to some other town nigh Newport, for the conveniency of transporting our families. In consequence of this advice we have employed Mr. Arnold,[2] a lawyer, to

1. The Committee of Safety for 1776 comprised Metcalf Bowler, John Cooke, John Smith, Daniel Tillinghast, John Northup, Joseph Stanton, Jr., William Bradford and Stephen Mumford. This body seems to have been first elected in 1775. Their powers were entirely undefined. Some such general power as was conferred in May, 1776. (*Acts and Resolves, May, 1776, p. 51*). They were to meet during the recess of the Assembly, "transact such business as the exigency of public affairs may require," advise His Honor the Governor as to their doings and make report to the next session. No reports by them appear in any printed records.

2. This was probably Jonathan Arnold, Esq., who at this time occupied a prominent position in Providence, and at a later period he represented Rhode

write one for each of us. These we have forwarded to Newport. That of mine I sent per D. Tillinghast,[1] to the care of my brother William,[2] which I desired might be presented and properly enforced by him and his friends. We had many gentlemen to see us this day, which we take very kindly. Nothing very material has occurred this day. The house is much crowded and in great confusion, which renders our lives disagreeable. But we keep our spirits as well as can be expected. Turned in at half after nine.

Thursday, September 12, 1776. Arose before six; while we were yet in bed John Smith, Esq.,[3]

Island in the Continental Congress. He was there accused of having disclosed the secrets of Congress to the enemies of his country. He denied the accusation, but immediately left Congress and soon after left the State.

1. Daniel Tillinghast was a member of the Committee of Safety; a resident of Providence.

2. William Vernon was a very prominent merchant, resident at Newport. He there prosecuted a large mercantile business in connection with his brother Samuel. They were both brothers of our Diarist, Thomas. William married Judith, daughter of Philip Hammond; she was the great-granddaughter of Deputy Governor Clarke and Governor John Cranston.

Samuel Vernon married Amey, daughter of Governor Richard Ward. He was thus the brother-in-law of Henry Ward, the Secretary of State.

These men all supported the cause of the Colonies, saving Thomas.

3. John Smith was very largely engaged in distilling rum in the neighbor-

sent his compliments, and desired to know our commands, being just going to Newport, which we take to be very kind. Samuel Gibbs,[1] an exile, who has been confined to the house, signed the Test yesterday, and took his passage for Newport this morning at ten o'clock. Nothing extraordinary has happened this day. We breakfast and dine at the common table, and make matters in every circumstance as agreeable as possible in this situation, hoping for better times soon. We keep good houses, and keep the house as quiet as we can. To bed at half after nine.

Friday, September 13, 1776. Arose at six and in good spirits. James Wyatt, Mrs. Beale, and Sally Hammett made us a visit at half after eight from Newport. All is well, and very good encouragement that we shall be released soon on good

hood of Providence during this period. He was a member of the Committee of Safety for 1776. As here stated, he offered his services to the prisoners while on his way to attend a session of the Committee, but on his return, September 14, paid them not even the courtesy of an answer to their appeal.

1. Samuel Gibbs was banished from Newport by the act of July, 1776. He was to be removed to Scituate and to be there confined to the portion of the town lying north of the Plainfield road. But Mr. Gibbs refusing to pay the sheriff the expense of his removal, he was committed to the jail in Providence.

terms. Mr. Wyatt returned to Newport. We had a piece of roast beef for dinner, the like I have not seen since I came from Newport. I dined heartily. Two or three persons have been to see us to-day, and Mrs. Beale, John Jenckes and his wife came in the evening and tarried till nine o'clock. We turned in before ten.

Saturday, September 14, 1776. Arose before six. Cloudy morning, and rainy the forepart of the day. We saw Samuel Chace upon the wharf.[1] Nothing worth remarking this forenoon. John Smith is returned from Newport, but it seems he don't care to speak to us. This day is very warm and sultry, which makes our quarters not very agreeable, as we are much crowded. In the evening our landlord, Mr. Beverley, returned from Newport. He tells us that the Committee disposed some of us to different places. But how and on what terms we cannot yet be informed. Nicholas Tillinghast, Mrs. Beale, Sally Hammett, Mr. Cozzens[2] and

1. The statement that one could look out of the jail windows and recognize persons on the wharves along the Cove seems difficult of realization, but in those days vessels of considerable draft discharged their cargoes along where Canal street now runs.

2. Matthew Cozzens, a citizen of Newport, was exiled by the act of July.

many others spent the evening with us. We retired
to bed at ten.

Sunday, September 15, 1776. Arose before six.
A calm, still morning. Nothing transpires this forenoon respecting us, Mr. Ward having not yet come
to town. After dinner three or four ship captains,
who have been captured, came to see us. This
afternoon James Wyatt came from Newport and
brought me letters from Mrs. Vernon and brother
William, advising me that the Committee had ordered me to Warwick under certain restrictions.[1]
Mrs. Beale and sundry other ladies and gentlemen
spent the evening with us. To bed at ten.

Monday, September 16, 1776. Arose about six.
Wrote a letter to Mrs. Vernon by young Jenkins.
Waited on Mr. Henry Ward; he was very kind and
genteel to me. Got my papers from his office, the

He was sentenced to Cumberland and was there taken. He does not seem
to have long remained there, but broke his parole and returned to Newport,
where he was again arrested and committed to the Providence Jail. He was
one of Mr. Vernon's subscribers to the Boston Chronicle.

  2. The editor has been unable to find what these restrictions were, but from
a letter to his brother it appears that one restriction was that he should not
reside nearer to the Cove at Apponaug than a half mile   This letter is printed
in full under the date of September 30. A further discussion of these restrictions appears under the date of September 19.

order of the Committee, &c. Signed my parole for the town of Warwick, and set out for said town in a chaise with Sally Hammett at four o'clock, after taking my leave of Mr. Beale and Mr. Nicol, whom I left in gaol.[1] We arrived at Warwick with a dull horse after eight o'clock. We stopped at the house of Mr. Thomas Wickes, whose family received me most joyfully. We tarried with them all night. They expressed a concern that I could not be with them until I provided myself with suitable lodgings. To bed after nine.

Tuesday, September 17, 1776. Arose before sunrise. The family not yet being up, I strayed up to Captain Warner's. He was glad to see me. I told him my state and circumstances. Staid to breakfast with him. We discussed on divers matters and things. Mrs. Joseph Lippitt[2] joined us. We tarried at this house to dinner; met with a hearty welcome. Sally Hammett called at three o'clock, on her way to

1. This is the last of Mr. Beale, but Mr. Nicol's name appears once more in the letter of September 30.

2. Mrs. Joseph Lippitt was the daughter of Captain Thomas Brown, of Rehoboth. She died May 20, 1795, a lady possessing a truly amiable character, beloved by all who knew her.

Providence. Captain Warner would not part with me. Tarried here this night, and went to bed soon after nine.

Wednesday, September 18, 1776. Arose at six. Pleasant morning. Walked in the fields till breakfast. I cannot be too thankful for this gentleman's civility. His conversation is agreeable and sensible, which makes me happy. Wrote a letter to Mrs. Vernon this afternoon per John Townsend.

Thursday, September 19, 1776. Arose about six. Took a turn in the fields before breakfast. Nathaniel Mumford[1] came to see us; had a good deal of conversation with him in respect to my limits, ordered by the Committee. He is privily of the opinion, and so is Captain Warner, that it could not have been the intention of the Committee, that I should not go into or reside in the street of the old town of Warwick; and that the cove cannot be considered as the seashore; and that were they in my situation they should not feel themselves in the least danger of forfeiting their parole were they to reside in that

---

1. Nathaniel Mumford was one of the Standing Committee appointed by the Assembly to examine accounts. He served the State in many ways, and seems to have possessed the confidence of his contemporaries.

street. But notwithstanding this opinion and advice I prefer at present to avoid censure. My mind is much uneasy, being conscious that Captain Warner's family is large, and that it must be a great inconveniency for him, for me to be at his house.

Friday, September 20, 1776. Arose with the sun. Walked in the fields. But my mind and thoughts are much discomposed. Mr. Mumford spent the day with us. Mr. Joseph Lippitt's son died last night. Wrote a letter to Mrs. Vernon by Quaco Johnston. The family treats me with all possible marks of respect. Nevertheless my mind is greatly agitated with regard to my situation.

Saturday, September 21, 1776. Arose with the sun, as usual. Took an airing in the fields which are pleasant and agreeable, although the weather is drizzly, and threatens a storm. The weather clears up in the afternoon. I have heard no news from home since my arrival here. I am still in an uneasy, unsettled situation, being sensible that I am an encumbrance to the family, but know not where to fix until I hear from Newport.

Sunday, September 22, 1776. Arose at sunrise.

10

Fine morning. I cannot say that I have been well since my arrival in this town; although I am better this morning, having walked the fields a good deal. The family are gone (at eleven o'clock) to Mr. Lippitt's funeral, which gives me leisure to write to Mrs. Vernon by Allen's boat, which sails for Newport in the morning. Mr. Graves and his brother called to see me this afternoon, and gave me a word of comfort. Sally Hammett called also. They all returned to Providence.

Monday, September 23, 1776. Arose as usual; walked in the fields some miles with Captain Warner and Mr. Mumford this forenoon. William Bardin and his brother called on their way to Providence. Brought a letter from Mrs. Vernon and some necessaries for me.

Tuesday, September 24, 1776. Cloudy morning and very cold, sour day. Nothing worth remarking. Presented Mrs. Warner with a canister of tea and a pound of chocolate.

Wednesday, September 25, 1776. Cool, clear morning; wind N. W. The forenoon, at eleven o'clock, I took my leave of this family, and went to the house of the W'd Greene, about half a mile farther eastward. Lodgings, one dollar and a half per week. The people are very kind.

Thursday, September 26, 1776. This morning is warmer; wind S. W. The day pleasant. At two o'clock P. M., Mr. Warner's nephew returned from Newport; he brought letters from Mrs. Vernon and brother Will, and other friends. I have liberty to go and reside in the street if I choose. He brought some clothes and necessaries for my comfort. Visited Captain Warner twice this day.

Friday, September 27, 1776. The weather much warmer; wind S. W. The family that I am at present with are very kind and obliging. Nothing worthy of notice this day.

Saturday, September 28, 1776. This day is cool and clear. N. E. wind. Bought half a gallon of rum for my comfort.

Sunday, September 29, 1776. Cloudy, windy day; wind S. E. Company to dine with me; the two Mr. Graves came to see me after dinner, and some other gentlemen and ladies.

Monday, September 30, 1776. A fresh wind at

S. W., but pleasant towards evening. This day has been employed in writing to my friends at Newport, Mrs. Vernon, brother William¹ and others. In the

" WARWICK. Sept. 30th. 1776.

1. " DEAR BROTHER :—I rec'd your kind, affectionate letter of the 14th at Providence and your last by Allen's boat; I should have answered the former in season, but being in an unsettled state rendered it almost impossible for me to compose my mind to write. A place offered about half a mile eastward of Captain Warner's. Could not possibly think of tarrying there any longer. Accordingly, on Wednesday last. shifted my lodgings to the house of the widow Green's. The family, tho' small, are exceeding kind and obliging, and much retired, being yet, I am told, above half a mile from the cove. Your explanation of that matter corresponds with the opinion of the people here, and indeed it was always my sentiments; and for this reason, if the Cove at Providence had been judged to be the Sea Shore, Messrs. Nicols & Cozzens had not been ordered to the bounds of the Elm Tree, which is much nearer that Cove than the street here is to this, besides being very publick.

" I thank you for your care in drawing the Petition anew; it was not done agreeable to my directions; I condemn'd it the moment I saw it, but being after Ten at night when I rec'd it, and the Gentleman going to Newport very early in the morning, had not time to draw it over, or even to make remarks; I was sorry afterwards that I sent it, but being in a place of much confusion and disorder, I hardly knew what I did. Would just hint that I was taken from my family (but whether with or

afternoon drank tea with Mrs. Wickes, and was
very kindly received.

without cause, is not at present the case, I am conscious that I
have given none) at a time very unexpectedly, when you may
suppose I left my affairs in a disordered state, which makes it
absolutely necessary for me to be at Newport a few days; I
mentioned this to Mr. Ward (whom to do justice was very genteel to me) and he made not the least doubt but this favor could
be obtained upon proper application; if you'll be kind eno'
to think of this matter, it will still lay me under further obligations. I thank you for ye Tea, it came very seasonably; it's true
Mrs. Vernon had before sent me a small canister, with some
chocolate, w'ch I could not avoid presenting to Mrs. Warner,
she is a really kind, good woman. I also thank you for every
instance of your kindness in soliciting in my behalf in this very
disagreeable business, and should still think myself under very
great obligations to the Legislative authority if I could be permitted to reside with my family under certain restrictions, but it
seems this cannot be the case consistent with the acts of Gover't;
must be content with my present lott, I had almost said hard, a
word which I have not lately frequently made use of.

"I do not know to what place our Sister Sanford is destined
these troublesome times, but wherever she may be, if you have
opport'y, do make my most affectionate regards and love to her,
Brother Sam'll, Sister Esther, and every branch of our family.
I wish you the highest degree of health and happiness with sin-
cerity, and are Yrs. &c.,

"T. VERNON."

"To Mr. William Vernon, Newport."

Tuesday, October 1, 1776. Agreeable day for the season. Forwarded my letters to Newport by Mr. Nat Mumford.

Wednesday, October 2, 1776. Cool morning; the wind northerly; sent a letter for Mr. Anthony to Henry Ward, Esq., and inclosed a petition to the Committee to be convened at Providence the third instant, desiring that I might have liberty to see my family a few days, and settle my affairs at Newport. Jeremiah Lippitt, Esq.,[1] made his exit this evening, about nine o'clock.

Thursday, October 3, 1776. Cool, cloudy morning; wind easterly. Visited Mrs. Mumford and Miss Godfrey this afternoon. Rained in the evening.

Friday, October 4, 1776. Thick, cloudy morning and rainy. The wind at N. E., and continued so during the whole day; nothing material.

1. Jeremiah Lippitt was a worthy citizen of Warwick. He was born January 27, 1711. Died October 2, 1776. He held the office of Town Clerk thirty-three years, from 1742 to his death in 1776. He married Welthian Greene, daughter of Richard Greene, September 12, 1734. His daughter Anne married Colonel Christopher Greene, and subsequently to his death, Colonel John Low.

Saturday, October 5, 1776. Cloudy, thick morning, and cold with rain. The wind N. E., but the weather cleared up very unexpectedly in the afternoon. At twelve o'clock attended Mr. Jeremiah Lippitt's funeral. At four o'clock received a letter from Henry Ward, Esq., advising me that the Committee had given me liberty to go to Newport for eight days to settle my affairs.

Sunday, October 6, 1776. Agreeable morning; little wind; northerly. Went to the south part of the town to inquire for a boat to go to Newport. But Allen was not returned from Providence. Wrote a letter to Mr. Ward, acknowledged the receipt of his letter, and thanked him for his kindness in presenting my petition.

Monday, October 7, 1776. A very pleasant, agreeable morning; very little wind; northerly. Heard that Allen's boat is come from Providence and intends for Newport in the morning. Prepared for the passage by sending my things to the boat.

Tuesday, October 8, 1776. A remarkably calm morning but cloudy. We set sail about nine o'clock in company with Mrs. Mumford and her son. The tide of ebb-being in our favor till eleven we got out of the cove, but continued calm till twelve o'clock, when the wind breezed up at about S. S. W. Arrived at my own house before six. Found my family and friends all well.[1]

1776.   MEMORANDUM OF EXPENSES IN JULY AND AUGUST.

Paid for eggs several times,	-	-	-	£0 2 3
One lb. tea, Mrs. Vernon (p'd),	-	-	-	10 0
Besides half a lb. brought with me (p'd for)				
Horse and chais to Warwick,	-	-	-	12 9
At Captain Warner's,	-	-	-	-	12 0
At Mrs. Greene's.				

1. By the following order of the Assembly, passed at the October session, 1776, all exiles were allowed to return to their homes:

"IT IS VOTED AND RESOLVED, That all those suspected persons who, by order of the Assembly, were removed from the town of Newport into other towns in this State have liberty to return to their own homes as soon as they please, first paying all the charges that have arisen from the time of their removal until their return; except Christopher Hargill,[2] who, not being able to pay the charge at present, is to give his note therefor." (Acts and Resolves, R. I. Gen. Assem., October, 1776, p. 9.)

2. Christopher Hargill was one of those banished by the act of July.

END OF THE DIARY.

THE

VERNON FAMILY AND ARMS,

A COMMUNICATION TO THE

NEW ENGLAND HISTORICAL AND GENEALOGICAL REGISTER, FOR
JULY, 1879,

BY

HARRISON ELLERY,

OF BOSTON, MASS.

WITH

ADDITIONS AND CORRECTIONS,

BY

THOMAS VERNON,

OF NEW YORK CITY.

THE VERNON FAMILY AND ARMS.

—— ◆ ———

WHEN the inscriptions and coats-of-arms on the tombstones in the old burying ground situated in the northern part of Newport, R. I., were copied for the Heraldic Journal, those bearing the arms of the Vernon family were overlooked; probably from the fact that the family lot is surrounded by a high arbor-vitæ hedge. Within this enclosure are many ancient and modern stones to different members of the family; the two oldest being to Daniel, the emigrant ancestor, and his wife Ann. The next in order are two large, broad, flat stones engraved with the Vernon arms, and bearing an inscription to the Hon. Samuel Vernon and his wife Elizabeth. They are dated 1737 and 1721–'22, respectively. Samuel was the son of Daniel, who came over from England and founded the American family of the name. Daniel was in possession of a seal ring bearing the same arms as those on the tombstones mentioned, which he inherited from his brother, Samuel Vernon, of London, whose widow sent it to him from England. The ring is now lost—but a good impression of it, from which the cut used in this Tract was engraved —is in the possession of Thomas Vernon, Esq., of the firm of Vernon & Hill, attorneys and counsellors at law, New York city. Mr. Vernon, who is the son of the late Hon. Samuel Brown Vernon, of Newport, formerly General Treasurer of Rhode Island, has furnished, at my solicitation, most of the material for this genealogy, and the affidavits from the originals in his possession.

It will be seen that the Vernon family is one of our few families who have always been able to trace the use of coat armor to their English ancestors.

The following affidavits were made to enable the Hon. Samuel Vernon, of Newport, son of Daniel, to assert his title to property in London, consisting of a range of warehouses on the Thames and Quay, which had been much injured by the fire, which, after the death of his father and his father's sister, he went over to England and diposed of.

The Deposition of Elisha Dyre of North Kingstown in the Colony of Rhode Island, &c., who being Duly Sworn Testifyeth and Saith —

That he was Personally Acquainted with Daniel Vernon Late of North Kingstown in the Colony Aforesaid, Now Deceased, and with some of his Sisters and his Brother Samuel Vernon's Widdow that Lived in the City of London, and Likewise with Samuel Vernon of Newport in Rhode Island, Esqr. Son to the S^d Daniel Vernon, which S^d Samuel Vernon he Knoweth of his Ceartaine Knowledge to be the only and Ligitimate Son of the Afore Named Daniel Vernon, and Further this Deponent Saith, that when he was in London the Widdow of the first Named Samuel Vernon Desired him to bring her Husbands Legacy of A Gold Ring to his Brother Daniel Vernon Afore Named, but he Refused it by Reason he was not A Coming Directly to New England, and She Sent it by John Scott to the Said Daniel Vernon and he Received it Accordingly to this Deponant Knowledge.

ELISHA DYRE.

11

The above Subscriber Elisha Dyre Personally Appeared in North Kingstown and made Solemn Oath to the Whole Truth of the Above Written Evidence the 15th Day of May A. D. 1736.

Before Christor Phillips, Justice Peace.

The Deposition of Hannah Place of North Kingstown in the Colony of Rhode-Island, &c. Who Being Duly Sworn Testifyeth and Saith—

That She was well Acquainted with Daniel Vernon Late of the Afore S^d North Kingstown, Butt now Desceas^d and his Wife Ann Vernon, And was Present and Saw them Married Togeather According to Law, and That to her Ceartaine Knowledge Samuel Vernon of Newport Esqre is the only and Legitimate Son of the Afore Named Daniel Vernon and Ann Vernon his Wife.

HANNAH PLACE.

The above Subscriber Hannah Place Personally Appeared in North Kingstown and made Oath to the Whole Truth of the Above Written Evidence the 15th Day of May A. D. 1736.

Before Christor Phillips, Justice Peace.

Daniel Updike of Newport in the County of Newport in the Colony of Rhode Island &c., Gentleman, Aged about forty two years, and being duly Sworn testifieth and Saith that about the Year 1715, One Daniel Vernon died at the Deponent's Fathers House in North Kingston after having lived for many

Years preceeding said Time at said Place as a Tutor to the Deponent's and to his Father's other Children. And the Depon' very well remembers that by the Account the said Daniel Vernon gave of himself and Family he was the Son of One Samuel Vernon of London and was himself born there, and that he had Two Brothers Inhabitants of that City, One named John Vernon and the other Samuel Vernon, the latter of which by the Relation given by said Daniel Vernon was drowned, And the said Daniel Vernon shewed me a Seal Ring being a Cornelion Stone cut with Three Wheat Sheaves the Arms born by the Family of Vernon, which was (as he said) his said Brother Samuels. Further the Depon' testifieth that a French Bible by him produced printed at Rochelle Anno 1616 was the Bible of the said Daniel Vernon, and by him left at his Death, and that the Hand Writing on the Back Side of a Leaf in said Bible on the other Side of which is the Command^mts (which Writing gives an Account in English of the Death of Samuel Vernon the said Daniel Vernon's Father, of John Vernon, of The said Daniel Vernon's Mother, and of Samuel Vernon his Brother,) the Depon' knoweth to be the Hand Writing of the said Daniel Vernon as perfectly as he knoweth any Writing that was not written in his Presence. And Further the Depon' saith he never knew or heard of

any Person besides the aforenamed Daniel Vernon
that bore that name Saving his Son who deceased
without Issue; Again the Depon[t] testifieth that he
well knoweth Samuel Vernon of Newport aforesaid
Esq[re] and that he is the Lawful Son and Heir of the
aforenamed Daniel Vernon (who died at the De-
pont's Fathers House as aforesaid) in the Accepta-
tion of Mankind in the Govern[t] where the Depon[t] liveth, which is also the Place where the said
Samuel Vernon liveth, is well known and Sustaineth
the Place of a Judge of the Superior Court of Judicature. Further the Depon[t] Saith not.

DANIEL UPDIKE.

Newport Rhode Island May 28th Anno 1736.

The within named Daniel Updike Gentleman, Personally Appeared before me the Subscriber one of his majesties Justices
of the Peace for the County of Newport, and made Solemn
Oath to the Truth of the within written Deposition, to which
had subscribed his name, and the Bible hereunto annexed is
the very Bible to him Referred to in S[d] Deposition. In Testimony whereof I have hereunto Set my hand and for the
Annexing S[d] Bible Affixed my Seal.

SAMUEL WICKHAM.

Katharine Updike of North Kingston in the
County of Kings County in the Colony of Rhode
Island, &c. Gentlewoman, being duly sworn testi-
fieth and saith that about the Year One thousand

seven hundred and fifteen, One Daniel Vernon died at the Dwelling House of the Depon[ts] Father in said North Kingston, at which Place the said Daniel Vernon had lived for many Years preceeding his Death. And the Depon[t] lived in the Same House with him for several Years, even until the Time of his Death, and hath often heard him give an Account of himself and Family. That he was born in London and that his Fathers name was Samuel Vernon. That he had had two Brothers Inhabitants of that City, One named John Vernon and one named Samuel Vernon. That they were both dead and that the latter of them was drowned a fishing in the New River, And the Depon[t] observed a Ring Worn by the said Daniel Vernon set with a Cornelion Stone cut with Three Wheat Sheaves which he said was the Arms of his Family and sent from England to him, And the Depon[t] saith that a French Bible printed at Rochelle, Anno 1616, was the Bible of the said Daniel Vernon, and by him given to the Depon[t] at his Death, And the Hand Writing on the Back Side of a Leaf in said Bible on the other side of which is the Commandments (which Writing gives an Account of the Death of Samuel Vernon the said Daniel Vernons Father, of John Vernon, of the said Daniel Vernon's mother, and of Samuel Vernon his Brother) The Depon[t] knoweth to be the

Writing of the said Daniel Vernon as well as She knoweth the writing of any Person, she being much acquainted with it. And further the Depon[t] saith not.

KATHARINE UPDIKE.

Newport Rhode Island May 28th 1736

Then the above named Mrs. Katharine Updike, Personally Appeared before me the Subscriber one of his majestics Justices of the Peace for the County of Newport, and made Solemn Oath to the Truth of the above written Deposition to w[h] She had Subscribed her name and the Bible hereunto Annexed is the Very Bible by her Referred to in S[d] Deposition. In Testimony whereof I have hereunto Subscribed my name and for the Annexing the Bible Affixed my Seal as aforesaid.

SAMUEL WICKHAM.

A certificate prefixed to these depositions, dated May 29, 1736, and signed by John Wanton, governor, and Jas. Martin, secretary of the colony of Rhode Island, certifies that Samuel Wickham, Esq., was then a justice of the peace in commission for the town of Newport, and that Christopher Phillips, Esq., was justice of the peace in commission for North Kingstown.

The bible of Daniel Vernon, referred to in the above affidavits, is now owned by Mrs. George Talbot Olyphant, of New York. It is in the French language, printed at Rochelle in 1616. It also contains the whole Book of psalms collected in English metre, London, 1629; also confession of faith, and so forth.

In this bible are the following entries in Daniel Vernon's handwriting:

My Hon⁴ Father Samuel Vernon Dyed the 25ᵗʰ day of April 1681—St. Marks day. My brother John Vernon Dyed April, 1682, 42 years of age, in London, on St. Marks day. My Hon⁴ Mother Dyed April 24ᵗʰ, 1701, Aged four score years the time the Queen was crowned.

My brother Samuel Vernon was drowned at ye New River a fishing 17ᵗʰ July, 1703, Aged 42 years.

Myself was born in London Sept 1ˢᵗ 1643.

My son Daniel Vernon was born the 6ᵗʰ day of April 1682, at one O'clock at Newport, Rhode Island.

My son Samuel Vernon was born the 6ᵗʰ day of December in the year 1683, in the day time at 8 o'clock at Narragansett.

I was married to my wife 22 Sept. at Narragansett 1679.

My daughter Catharine was born the 3ᵈ day of Oct. Sabbath day, two hours before day break at Rhode Island in the year 1686.

Mr. Vernon, who made the above extracts from the bible twelve or fifteen years ago, thinks that he paid no attention to the ancient mode of spelling or use of capitals at that time.

1. SAMUEL[1] VERNON, had children :

    i.   JOHN, b. about 1640; d. April, 1682, a. 42.
2. ii. DANIEL, b. Sept. 1, 1643.
   iii. SAMUEL, b. about 1661; d. July 17, 1703, a. 42.

2. DANIEL[2] VERNON (*Samuel[1]*), born in London, Eng., Sept. 1, 1643, is said to have come to this country about the year 1666. His emigration is thought to have been in part determined from the losses his father sustained in the great fire of that year in London; a range of his warehouses on the Thames and Quay having been burned in that disastrous fire. Mr. Vernon had received a very superior education; spoke several languages, and was long a tutor in the family of Lodowick Updike, of North Kingstown, R. I. In 1683 he was clerk of Kingston; also constable. In 1686 he was appointed marshal of Kings province and keeper of the prison; in 1687, with Henry Tibbets, he was appointed to lay out certain highways in Rochester. In 1687, he was also a selectman of Rochester.* On his arrival

---

* In June, 1686, Edmund Randolph came into the King's Province under a

from England he appears to have first resided at Newport, but shortly removed to Narragansett, where at Tower Hill, Sept. 22, 1679, he married Ann Dyre, a widow, daughter of Capt. Edward Hutchinson, Jr., and granddaughter of the celebrated Anne Hutchinson, and grand neice of John Dryden. She died Jan. 10, 1716; her gravestone is still standing in the family lot at Newport, beside that of her husband. He died Oct. 28, 1715. Children:

> i. DANIEL, b. April 6, 1682; d. young, probably in infancy.
>
> 3. ii. SAMUEL, b. Dec. 6, 1683.
>
> iii. CATHERINE, b. Oct. 3, 1686; d. unm. March, 1769.

3. SAMUEL³ VERNON (*Daniel*,² *Samuel*¹), born Dec. 6, 1683; m. April 10, 1707, by Nathaniel Coddington, Esq., to Elizabeth Fleet, of Long Island. He became a distinguished citizen of Newport; was an assistant from 1729 till his death in 1737, and a judge of the superior court of judicature. In 1737, he was one of the commissioners appointed to fix the disputed boundary line between Massachusetts and New Hampshire. His constant

---

commission from the King, held a court, and amongst other things, changed the names of the three towns which the Province contained—Kingstown was called Rochester, Westerly was called Haversham, and Greenwich was called Dedford. The former names were restored in 1689.

election to office shows that he was highly esteemed in the community, and he doubtless would have attained still further distinction had not his useful career been arrested by his death, Dec. 5, 1737, while still in the prime of life. Mrs. Vernon died March 5, 1721-2, æ. 37 years. Their gravestones, bearing the family arms, are still in the Newport cemetery. Children:

i. ANN, b. Jan. 23, 1707-8; d. Sept. 23, 1782; m. Mr. Sanford; had one son Samuel, secretary of the Newport Insurance Co.

ii. ELIZABETH, b. Aug. 4, 1709; m. Capt. Elnathan Hammond, of Newport, merchant; had a still-born son July 21, 1753.

4. iii. SAMUEL, b. Sept. 6, 1711.

iv. ESTHER, b. Aug. 20, 1713; spinster.

v. DANIEL, b. Aug. 20, 1716; freeman 1738. He lived and died a bachelor.

vi. THOMAS, b. May 31, 1718; m. Sept. 9, 1741, Jane, dau. of John Brown, merchant, of Newport. She d. April 28, 1765, æ. 43 yrs. He next m. May 20, 1766, Mary Mears, who d. Aug. 1787. He was a merchant of the firm of Grant & Vernon; was royal postmaster at Newport from 1745 to 1775; register of the court of vice-admiralty twenty years; secretary of the Redwood Library, and senior warden of Trinity Church. He was a tory, the only one of the family, and suffered about four months imprisonment on account of his tory principles. He wrote a journal of his captivity, now in possession of the Newport Historical Society.

His house was on the west side of Division Street. He died May 1, 1784, without issue.

5. vii. WILLIAM, b. Jan. 17, 1719.
   viii. MARY, b. Dec. 23, 1721; d. May 17, 1770, a spinster.

4. SAMUEL⁴ VERNON (*Samuel,*³ *Daniel,*² *Samuel*¹), born Sept. 6, 1711; m. Amey, daughter of Governor Richard Ward. She d. Jan. 17, 1792, in her 75th year. He was a prominent Newport merchant; long a member of the house of S. & W. Vernon. He was one of the original applicants for the charter of the Redwood Library; and, in 1750, was one of the petitioners to the King to restrain the Legislature from issuing bills of credit. His house was the old Olyphant house on Church Street, still owned by his descendant, Mrs. E. De W. Thayer. He died July 6, 1792. Their gravestones are standing. Children:

   i. ELIZABETH, b. April 24, 1738; m. Capt. Valentine Whightman; had one child, Mary, d. May, 1840.

   ii. WILLIAM, b. Aug. 3, 1739; died the following Saturday night.

   iii. SAMUEL, b. July 12, 1740; died Aug. 23, 1741.

   iv. AMEY, b. Sept. 12, 1741; d. Aug. 28, 1742.

   v. MARY, b. Feb. 17, 1742-3; m. Nov. 26, 1760, Christopher Ellery, an eminent merchant of Newport and a revolutionary patriot. He was a son of Deputy Gov. William Ellery, and brother of William Ellery, one of the signers of the Declaration of Independence. He was Deputy in the Colonial

Assembly, a Judge of the County Court, and an
Assistant of the Colony. He was chairman of the
committee of arrangement appointed by the town
of Newport to receive Washington on the occasion of his first visit to Newport, and entertained
the distinguished guest at his residence. Children:—1. *Elizabeth Almy[6] Ellery*, b. March 24,
1764.   2. *Benjamin[6] Ellery*.   3. *Christopher[6] Ellery*,* b. Nov. 1, 1768.   4. *Samuel[6] Ellery*, b.
Sept. 29, 1770.   5. *Mary[6] Ellery*, b. May 15, 1772;
married Asher Robbins, U. S. Senator for R. I.,
1825–1839.   6. *Margaret[6] Ellery*, b. June 17, 1775;
d. Dec., 1775.

6. vi.   SAMUEL, b. Feb. 17, 1744–5; d. Dec. 1, 1809.

vii.   AMEY, b. July 19, 1746; d. Aug. 18, 1746.

viii.   AMEY, b. Nov. 19, 1747; m. Samuel King, portrait
painter; instructor of Allston and Malbone. Children:—1. *Samuel[6] King*, an eminent merchant, of
New York, who as early as 1803, and probably
earlier, was head of the house of King & Talbot.

---

*Mr. Ellery served Rhode Island as one of her Senators in Congress from
1801 to 1805. In connection with his political life there is a curious anecdote
which very well illustrates the spirit of the time. It was in May, 1788, while
both houses of the R. I. General Assembly were joined in Grand Committee,
as is usual every year for the election of minor State officers, that Mr. Ellery,
not then a member, made some ill-natured, perhaps intemperate, remark
which reached the ears of this august body, and which they deemed deroga-
tory to their dignity, whereupon they passed the following resolution:

"WHEREAS, Christopher Ellery, Jun., of Newport, did on the seventh day
of this current month of May, when both houses of this Assembly were in
session in a Grand Committee, openly insult the Authority of this State;
and a warrant having been issued against him, and he brought before this
Assembly, and having pleaded guilty;

"IT IS VOTED AND RESOLVED, That the Sheriff of the County of Newport
take his body into custody, and him safely secure in close confinement in the
common Gaol in Newport, without bail or mainprize, until the further orders
of this Assembly." (*Acts and Resolves, May, 1788, p. 4.*)

He m. his cousin Harriet, dau. of Samuel Vernon.
2. *William Vernon⁶ King*, bachelor, lawyer, graduate of Brown University.

ix. WILLIAM, b. July 21, 1749; d. September, 1749.

x. WILLIAM WARD, b. March 7, 1752; d. in Jamaica, W. I., April 10, 1774.

xi. ANN, one of the sprightliest wits of Newport colonial society; b. Sept. 29, 1754; m. Oct. 23, 1786, Dr. David Olyphant, a Scottish gentleman whose devotion to the Stuart cause, sealed at Culloden, compelled his emigration to America. He went first to Charleston, S. C. On the breaking out of the Revolution he espoused the patriotic cause, and became medical director of the armies of the Carolinas, under Generals Gates and Greene. He was a member of the Rhode Island branch of the Society of the Cincinnati. Children:—1. *Ann⁶ Olyphant*, b. Oct. 27, 1787; spinster, who died in 1861 or 2 at Salem, N. C. 2. *David W. C.⁶ Olyphant*, born March 7, 1789; an eminent merchant of New York, head of the great

At a little later period during the same session the Assembly passed the following resolution of forgiveness:

"WHEREAS, Mr. Christopher Ellery, Jun., who was committed to Gaol for a contempt offered to this Assembly, and he being here brought, confesseth his fault, and puts himself upon mercy, and himself intreats pardon and forgiveness;

"IT IS THEREFORE VOTED AND RESOLVED, That the said Christopher Ellery, Jun., be forgiven; and that he be discharged upon his paying all costs." (*Acts and Resolves, May, 1788, p. 15.*)

By a turn in political affairs this same Grand Committee sent the man whom they sent to prison to the United States Senate. If any argument was needed to show that a political body like the Rhode Island Assembly was unfit to be entrusted with judicial power it can readily be found in this anecdote, nevertheless for two centuries they exercised it. If the Assembly sent every one to the prison, who, in these days denounced it, there would be few men left at liberty.

house of Olyphant & Co., China, and of Talbot.
Olyphant & Co., of New York. His grandson,
Talbot Olyphant, son of his son David, is now a
member of this house, and resides in New York,
having lately returned from China. Mr. Olyphant
m. Mrs. Archer, a widow; he died at Cairo,
Egypt, in June, 1851.

  xii. THOMAS, b. June 6, 1753; d. April 6, 1755.

5. WILLIAM⁴ VERNON (*Samuel,*³ *Daniel,*² *Sam-
uel¹*), born Jan. 17, 1719; m. Judith, dau. of Philip
Harwood, and great-granddaughter of Gov. Walter
Clarke and Gov. John Cranston, of Rhode Island.
She died Aug. 29, 1762, æ. 38 years. He died Dec.
22, 1806. Their graves are marked in the family
lot; his by a marble monument, hers by a stone.
Mr. Vernon's house was at the corner of Clarke and
Mary streets, and is still standing, a fine specimen
of colonial architecture. It has an historical interest, Mr. Vernon having given the gratuitous use of
it to the Count de Rochambeau during the Revolution, and hither Gen. Washington repaired on his
first visit to Newport. Mr. Vernon was one of the
most distinguished of the Newport merchants, and
one of the most self-sacrificing patriots of the Revolution. His trade extended to all the maritime
nations of Europe, the West Indies and Africa. He
lost eight vessels by capture in or about the year
1758. So conspicuous was he as a merchant, that

in 1778 a French house in Bordeaux solicited his patronage, and spoke of him as "universally known all over the continent of America." He contributed a vessel to the expedition against Louisburg. In 1773 the Colonial Assembly of Rhode Island appointed him one of a committee of three to prepare a letter to "his Majestie's Secretary of State" upon "the endangerment by a bill then pending in the House of Commons, of the fisheries prosecuted by R. I. merchants in and near the Gulf of St. Lawrence." He early espoused the patriot cause, and became a most unflinching "Son of Liberty." His great abilities as a merchant, and extensive acquaintance with marine affairs, enabled him at a very early period to assist Congress by his counsel. In 1774 he was appointed one of the committee of correspondence of the town of Newport, with the town of Boston. In 1775 he was appointed by the General Assembly, with William Ellery and others, a committee to collect statistics in regard to losses inflicted upon Rhode Island by the ministerial forces. In this year one of his vessels, the brig Royal Charlotte, was seized by Wallace in Newport harbor, taken to Boston and confiscated with its cargo. In 1776, when the British occupied Newport, he was forced to leave the place. May 6, 1777, he was elected by Congress one of the Continental Navy

Board, established at Boston, and was the president of the board from its organization to its dissolution. He not only gave his services without charge to his country, but advanced large sums to the government, which were only in part paid. His two colleagues in the navy board were James Warren and John Deshon, of Massachusetts. Of his losses he thus speaks under date of Oct. 10, 1778, in a letter to Josiah Hewes: "Mammon is no idol of mine. If we establish our rights and liberties upon a firm and lasting basis on the winding up of this bloody contest, I am content; altho' I own, if I could come at the property our enemies are possessed of, belonging to me, it would increase the pleasure. I do assure you it is no less a sum than twelve thousand pounds sterling at least, besides my real estate at Newport; yet I can with truth say it never broke my rest a moment." At the close of the war he reëntered upon commercial pursuits, and was one of the founders of the Newport Bank, of which institution his son Samuel and his grandson William were successively presidents. He was also one of the founders of the Newport Artillery Company in 1741. He was a great friend of learning, and assisted Dr. Witherspoon in raising funds for Princeton College. On the death of Abraham Redwood, he was elected the second president of the Redwood Library. He was on terms of affectionate intimacy with La Fayette, Dr. Stiles, Adams and Franklin; and was intimate with Jefferson, Viscount de Noailles, and other prominent men too numerous to mention.

His correspondence during colonial, revolutionary and post-revolutionary times, which is very large and well preserved, is in possession of Thomas Vernon, Esq., of New York, who contemplates printing it at some future day. He has also a large family correspondence of the Wards, Ellerys and Vernons of the same periods, which throws a good deal of light upon colonial times and life, and upon the feelings which permeated the men and women immediately before, during and after the Revolution.

Mr. George C. Mason, of Newport, in 1853, contributed a serial sketch of Mr. Vernon to the Newport Mercury.

William Vernon was a man of very imposing presence and courtly manners. Children :

7.   i. SAMUEL, b. May 29, 1757.

     ii. WILLIAM, b. March 6, 1759; d. unm. in 1833. He was afterwards known as William H. Vernon; was for many years secretary of the Redwood Library. He was a man of elegant and courtly manners, and was known in Newport as " Count Vernon." He graduated at Princeton College in 1776. He is famous as the owner of a celebrated collection of paintings of great merit, which he

made in France; an account of them is given in
the Galaxy of December, 1876. It is thought that
he may have inherited the seal ring referred to in
the affidavits, which may have been lost by him,
as while in France he went through many vicissi-
tudes. He was a constant and favored guest at
the court circles of Louis XVI., and a favorite of
the Queen.

At one time during the French Revolution he
was recognized as a courtier by the mob, dragged
to a lamp-post, and was only rescued from being
hanged by a Frenchman who knew him and assured the mob that he was an American citizen.

iii. PHILIP HARWOOD, b. April 3, 1761; d. Aug. 26,
1762.

6. SAMUEL[5] VERNON (*Samuel*,[4] *Samuel*,[3] *Daniel*,[2] *Samuel*[1]), b. Feb. 17, 1744–5; d. Dec. 1,
1809. He had two children :

   i. HARRIET, m. her cousin Samuel King.
   ii. WILLIAM S., of Louisville, Ky., who m. America
      Fontaine, and had :—1. *George Talbot*,[7] m. Mary
      Ross.   2. *Charles Fontaine*,[7] dead.   3. *Mary
      Ann*.[7] m. Nathaniel Wolfe, a distinguished lawyer
      of Louisville.   4. *Ann M.*[7]   5. *Harriet King*.[7]   6.
      Daniel Smith.[7]   7. *William S.*[7] dead.   8. *Edward
      Harwood*.[7]   9. *Grace*,[7] m. Francis L. B. Noad, of
      Montreal, Can.

7. SAMUEL[5] VERNON (*William*,[4] *Samuel*,[3] *Daniel*,[2] *Samuel*[1]), b. May 29, 1757 ; m. Dec. 31, 1784,
his cousin Elizabeth Almy, daughter of Christopher

and Mary (Vernon) Ellery. She was born March 24, 1764; died Feb. 21, 1857, æ. 93. Mr. Vernon was an eminent Newport merchant, and at one time its wealthiest citizen; was the first president of the Newport Bank, and president of the Rhode Island Insurance Company. During the Revolution he carried on business at Boston, where his father was discharging his official duties. He fought as a volunteer under Gen. Sullivan at the battle of Rhode Island, August, 1778, and his tomb was decorated with flowers on the centennial celebration of that battle. He died Nov. 22, 1834. Children:

   i. MARY, b. July 21, 1786; d. Feb. 14, 1787, unm.

  ii. CATHERINE, b. July 7, 1787; d. May 20, 1871; m. Rev. Joel Mann.

 iii. WILLIAM, b. Sept. 4, 1788; d. Dec. 18. 1867; m. first, Eliza D'Wolf, of Bristol, R. I.; m. second, Elizabeth Bryan, of Charleston, S. C.

 iv. Daughter. b. Sept. 15, 1789; d. Sept. 22, 1789.

  v. MARY, b. Jan. 3, 1792; d. July 16, 1811, unm.

 vi. EDWARD, b. Sept. 8, 1793; d. Feb. 12, 1861; m. Anna, dau. of Hon. Jabez Clark, Judge of Windham County, Conn.

 vii. ELIZABETH ALMY, b. April 28, 1795; d. Feb., 1816.

viii. PHILIP HARWOOD, b. Dec. 4, 1796: d. Sept 16, 1834, unm.

 ix. THOMAS, b. Dec. 20, 1797; d. May, 1876; m. Adelaide Augusta, dau. of John Winthrop, of Boston.

  x. Daughter, b. 1799; d. next day.

xi. SAMUEL BROWN, b. April 27, 1802; d. May 29, 1858; m. Oct. 26, 1830, Sophia, daughter of Joseph Peace, lawyer of Philadelphia.

The arms borne by the American family correspond with those of the noble family of Vernon in England, viz.: Or on a fesse az. three garbs of the field. Crest, A demi Ceres affrontée ppr. vested vert holding three ears of wheat over her left shoulder or, and in her right hand a sickle ppr., handle or. These arms are accorded by Burke to representatives of Richard de Vernon, who accompanied William the Conqueror to England, and was created, by Hugh Lupus, baron of Shipbrook, county of Chester.

Genealogical research in England may possibly connect Samuel of London, the ancestor of our Vernons, with this family.

GENEALOGY

FAMILY OF RICHARD GREENE,

POTOWOMUT.

BY

GEORGE SEARS GREENE.

FAMILY OF RICHARD GREENE,

OF POTOWOMUT.

— ◆ —

FIRST GENERATION IN NEW ENGLAND.

JOHN GREENE, surgeon, of Salisbury, Wiltshire, England; d. in Warwick, Jan., 1658-9; m. Joanne Tattershall, Nov. 4, 1619. Fourth child, Thomas Greene.

SECOND.

THOMAS GREENE, of Stone Castle, Old Warwick, R. I. Baptized in St. Thomas's Church, Salisbury, England, June 4, 1628; d. 5 June, 1717; buried at Stone Castle, Old Warwick; m. Elizabeth, dau. of Rufus Barton, June 30, 1659. Thomas, d. June 5, 1717. Second child, Thomas Greene.

THIRD.

THOMAS GREENE, of Potowomut, born Aug. 14, 1662, at Stone Castle; m. Anne, dau. of Major

John Greene, of Occupessnatuxet;* May 27, 1686. Anne, born March 19, 1662–3 ; died 1713. Thomas was drowned in going from Newport to Warwick, 1698–9 His father gave him the farm at Potowomut. Third child, John Greene.

FOURTH.

JOHN GREENE, of Potowomut, born April 14, 1691 ; d. 8 Dec., 1757 ; m. Deborah, dau. of Caleb Carr, of Jamestown, Dec. 6, 1721. Deborah d. May 6, 1729 ; m. second, Almy, dau. of Richard Greene, of Occupessnatuxet, Jan. 28, 1730–1. Seventh child, Richard Greene.

FIFTH.

RICHARD GREENE, born October 4, 1725 ; d. 19 June, 1779 ; m. Sarah, dau. of Thomas and Mary [Greene] Fry. Richard died July 17, 1779. Sarah died April 4, 1775.

Their children were :

SIXTH.

i. JOHN, b. March 22, 1746–7; d. Oct. 14, 1778; m. Barbara, dau. of Randall Holden, Sept. 30, 1770.

---

*Occupessnatuxet, this farm now occupied by the heirs of Gov. John Brown Francis, was purchased of Miantonomey, the Indian Chief, in Nov., 1642, by John Greene, surgeon, whose descendants occupied it till 6 Oct., 1782, when it was sold to John Brown, of Providence, whose descendents, the heirs of Gov. John Brown Francis, now occupy it. Like most Indian names, there seems to be several ways of spelling this one. Parsons gives it Occupasspatucket. On Walling's map it is Occu Pus Pawtuxet. The name appears to have been given to a cove.

ii. NATHANIEL, b. 31 July, 1748; m. Elizabeth, dau. of Henry Quincey, of Boston (in 1769) ; she d. 1781.

iii. WELTHYAN, b. Nov. 17, 1749; d. Jan. 6, 1753.

iv. THOMAS, b. Jan. 10, 1750; d. March 19, 1756.

v. SAMUEL, b. Aug. 8, 1752; d. Aug 10, 1761.

vi. WILLIAM, b. July 9, 1754; m. Dorothy Carlton, of South Carolina; d. 1786, without issue.

vii. MARY, b. Oct. 4, 1756; m. 22 Oct., 1787, Samuel Brown.

viii. ANNE, b. Aug. 17, 1758; d. May 4, 1759.

ix. SARAH, b. May 10, 1760; d. Nov. 11, 1820; m. Daniel Howland, Jr., Aug. 7, 1793.

x. ELIZABETH, b. Dec. 23, 1761; d. March 16, 1815; m. Sylvester G. Hassard, son of Robert, of South Kingstown and Coventry, March 5, 1786.

xi. BENJAMIN, b. Sept. 28, 1763.

xii. JOB, b. Nov. 22, 1765; d. at sea, 1810; m. —— Hewinson; no issue.

xiii. CALEB, b. Sept. 15, 1767; d. about 1832; m. —— Robinson, of Alexandria, Va.; issue, two sons and a daughter. The latter m. Rev. —— Gills, a clergyman of the Episcopal Church.

xiv. SAMUEL, b. Dec. 12, 1769; d. 1827; m. Henrietta Daniels, of Newport, Sept. 30, 1790; she d. 26 Sept., 1854.

SEVENTH.

CHILDREN OF
JOHN AND BARBARA [HOLDEN] GREENE.

i. RICHARD, d. in infancy.

ii. THOMAS, b. 20 July, 1772; d. 9 Nov., 1778.

iii. JOHN MALBONE, b. 3 May, 1774; d. Oct., 1817; m. 14 Feb., 1795, Anne, dau. William and Waite [Lockwood] Greene, of Old Warwick.

13

iv. SARAH, b. 4 July, 1776; d. 6 July, 1837; unm.
v.   MARY, b. 22 May, 1779; unm., living in Providence in
     1881, aged 102 years

CHILDREN OF

NATHANIEL AND ELIZABETH [QUINCY] GREENE.

i.   MARY, b. Dec. 18, 1769; d. unm.
ii.   RICHARD, b. Feb. 29, 1772; d. unm. Removed to
      Marietta, Ohio, with General Varnum.
iii. HENRY, b. May 26, 1773; m. Deborah Kell. He was a
      ship master, and died while in command of his ves-
      sel, buried in Trinity Church Yard, Dublin Ireland.
iv.   SALTER, d. unm.
v.   SARAH FRY, b. 15 Aug., 1778; d. 6 Jan., 1861; m. 21
      Dec., 1797, Thomas Cotterell, son of Thomas, of
      Newport, who was b. 1 Sept., 1772; died 3 Sept.,
      1848.

CHILDREN OF

SAMUEL AND MARY [GREENE] BROWN.

i.   JOB, b. 28 June, 1789; died 11 Sept., 1829.
ii.   LYDIA GREENE, b. 24 July, 1791; m. James LeBarron,
      of Bristol; no surviving issue.
iii. SUSAN, b. 28 June, 1789; d. 9 Nov., 1843.
iv.   SARAH, b. 27 Feb., 1795; d. unm.

CHILDREN OF

DANIEL AND SARAH [GREENE] HOWLAND.

i.   DEBORAH, b. July 8, 1795.
ii.   DAVID, b. Jan. 2, 1797.
iii. RICHARD, b. April 20, 1799.
iv.   ANNE, b. Feb. 20, 1801.

CHILDREN OF

SYLVESTER AND ELIZABETH [GREENE] HASSARD.

i. RICHARD.
ii. HENRY.
iii. LUKE.
iv. JOB
v. ROBERT, d. young.
vi. HANNAH.
vii. ELIZABETH.
viii. ESTHER.
ix. SAMUEL.
x. ABBY.

CHILDREN OF

SAMUEL AND HENRIETTA [DANIELS] GREENE.

i. BENJAMIN, b. Nov. 14, 1793; d. April 9, 1858; m. Lucy Beemis, of Pawtuxet; she d. Feb. 5, 1865.
ii. CALEB, b. Feb. 19, 1795; m. Mary Gray, of Tiverton, R. I.; m. second, Sarah Westcott.
iii. JOB, b. July 9, 1796; went to Java, East Indies, and married there.
iv. RICHARD, b. Aug. 23, 1798; d. Sept. 2, 1798.
v. MARY HENRIETTA, b June 21, 1799; m. John Taber.
vi. PETER, b. Feb. 11, 1801; m. Lydia Kent.
vii. JOHN DANIELS, b. April 30, 1805; m. Eliza Kent.

EIGHTH.

CHILDREN OF

John Malbone and Ann [Greene] Greene.

i. Sarah Ann, b. 22 Aug., 179—; d. unm.
ii. Celia, b. 18 Oct., 1800; m. Thomas Metcalf, of Macon, Ga.; his dau.. Eliza Rogers, m. Robert Kerr, of Georgia.
iii. A child, b. 2, and d. 3 Sept., 1803.
iv. William Amos, b. 1 March, 1807; m. Maria Louisa, dau. of Thomas Jacobs; his dau. Annie m. William Henry Owen, son of George Owen, of Providence, Oct. 22, 1872.

CHILDREN OF

Henry and Deborah [Kell] Greene.

i. Henry Quincy, b. 13 May, 1800; d. 10 July, 1830; m. Maria, dau. of Joel Herbert Bedell; she d. 12 Oct., 1876; issue 1, Angelina; 2, Maria Louisa; 3, Henry.

CHILDREN OF

Thomas and Sarah [Greene] Cotterell.

i. Anna Elizabeth; m. first, Bailey; m. second, Payne; issue by second marriage, Eloise Elizabeth; m. Rev. Lea Luquer; issue 1, Eloise Payne; 2, Lea McIlvane; 3, Thatcher Taylor Payne.
ii. Thomas Benjamin; d. unm.
iii. Joseph Swinburn; m.; no issue.
iv. Hannah Hopkins; d. in infancy.

CHILDREN OF

BENJAMIN AND LUCY [BEEMIS] GREENE.

i. MARY HENRIETTA, b. Aug. 27, 1816; m. Sept. 2, 1840. to Orville Coe.

ii. BARNABAS BUMP (Rev.), b. Aug. 31, 1818; m. May 17, 1841, to Nancy Caldwell Valandigham.

iii. SAMUEL CURTIS, b. July 2, 1822; m. June 16, 1847, to Eliza Hurd.

iv. ELIZABETH BARROWS, b. May 26, 1824; m. May 30, 1844, to Simon Lowderslayer.

v. BENJAMIN DANIELS, b. June 11, 1827; m. Sept. 30, 1846, to Laura Leavitt.

CHILDREN OF

CALEB AND MARY [GRAY] GREENE.

i. MARY ELIZA; m. Eben Joy.

Caleb Greene m. second, Sarah Westcott.

CHILDREN.

ii. RICHARD; m. Elizabeth Hatch.
iii. REUBEN.
iv. WILLIAM; m. Belle Collins.
v. LLOYD.
vi. SARAH; m. Limerick Harthman.
vii. MARTHA.

CHILDREN OF

JOHN AND MARY [GREENE] TABER.

i. MARY.
ii. JOHN.
iii. JAMES.
iv. ANN.

CHILDREN OF

PETER AND LYDIA [KENT] GREENE.

i. ADELINE; m. Charles Earl Carpenter, of Providence.

CHILDREN OF

JOHN DANIELS AND ELIZA [KENT] GREENE.

i. ELIZABETH; m. Charles Dickermore.
ii. WALTER.

FINIS.